W9-CCR-077

Elliott Roosevelt's™
MURDER
AT THE
PRESIDENT'S
DOOR

Also by Elliott Roosevelt

Murder in the Lincoln Bedroom
Murder in Georgetown
Murder in the Map Room
Murder at Midnight
Murder in the Château
Murder in the Executive Mansion
A Royal Murder
Murder in the East Room
New Deal for Death
Murder in the West Wing
Murder in the Red Room
The President's Man
A First-Class Murder
Murder in the Blue Room
Murder in the Rose Garden
Murder in the Oval Office
Murder at the Palace
A White House Pantry Murder
Murder at Hobcaw Barony
The Hyde Park Murder
Murder and the First Lady

Perfect Crimes (ed.)

Elliott Roosevelt's™

MURDER
AT THE
PRESIDENT'S
DOOR

An Eleanor Roosevelt Mystery

by William Harrington
for the Estate of Elliott Roosevelt

THOMAS DUNNE BOOKS
St. Martin's Minotaur
New York

THOMAS DUNNE BOOKS.
An imprint of St. Martin's Press.

ISBN 0-312-27499-8

Elliott Roosevelt's™

MURDER
AT THE
PRESIDENT'S
DOOR

I

IT WAS THE BEST of times, it was the worst of times. Etc. President Franklin D. Roosevelt had arrived in Washington with little to offer except his ebullient personality and his infectious optimism—as he was first to admit to the people in whom he confided: his wife, for one; also Louis McHenry Howe, his closest adviser; Harry Hopkins, another close friend and adviser; and his personal and private secretary, Marguerite "Missy" LeHand.

Mrs. Roosevelt, entering the White House to live there, found the place dismaying. The unhappy fact was, it was shabby. Carpets were worn through; drapes in some rooms were faded, and some were in shreds; furniture was in ill repair; the kitchen was inadequately equipped. Floors creaked. In some places they seemed to yield as one walked across them. The roof leaked, and some of the walls were streaked from water running down.

The trouble was that successive presidents had been reluctant to demand of Congress the large appropriations necessary to restore the building. Right now, in the depths of a depression that had left hundreds of thousands of men out of work and their families reduced to penury, with businessmen literally reduced to selling apples on the streets and farmers losing their land to foreclosures . . . now was not the time for the president to go to Congress and say that millions of dollars were needed to restore the White House.

Besides . . . there was a widespread impression all across America that the Roosevelts of Hyde Park were an immensely wealthy family who could afford at least to buy pots and pans for the White House kitchen and new drapes, for the family quarters anyway, and to furnish their living quarters in the style to which they were accustomed. Herbert and Lou Hoover had done just that, after all.

The impression was totally wrong. The president's mother had inherited the estate of his late father. It afforded her a comfortable living at Hyde Park, by no means a luxurious one.

Her son Franklin had cost Sara Roosevelt a great deal of money. His polio had rendered him for several years unable to make a living. He had practiced law in New York City, without earning any very large amount. She had to subsidize him—pay him an allowance—until he was elected governor of New York.

Now he was president of the United States. To Americans, many of whom were living on less than one hundred dollars a month, the presidential salary of twenty-five thousand dollars—on which he paid income tax like everyone else—seemed huge. The salary would not sustain him as a president had to be sustained in the White House, and his mother still had to extend help.

One of the problems was that it was a long-standing tradition in the White House that not only the members of the Secret Service detail but also the members of the press corps ate from the White House kitchen. There was a twenty-five-thousand-dollar appropriation for travel and entertainment—meaning chiefly state dinners—but the daily food bill was to be paid by the president, from his salary.

The living quarters were, to say the least, eccentric. Located on the second floor of the White House, they occupied the West Wing. A long central hall ran the entire length of the house, from west to east. The focus of the living quarters was what was known as the West Sitting Hall. This was the First Family's living room. Two rooms to the south became Mrs. Roosevelt's study and her bedroom. Two rooms to the north were guest rooms, for family visits.

The hall continued east in what was called the Center Hall. A room to the south of that was the president's bedroom. East of that room was a large oval room that became the president's study.

All of these rooms except the oval room had to be furnished by what the Roosevelts brought with them from their New York town house or from Hyde Park. The furnishings were therefore assorted and not matched.

Lou Hoover had achieved a degree of elegance in the living quarters, but she had taken her furniture with her when she left.

President Roosevelt immediately established a tradition that would last as long as his presidency: a cocktail hour in the West Sitting Hall at the end of the day. Coming up on a balky elevator from the Oval Office, he would wheel himself into the Sitting Hall and call out, "Who's home?"

Always home, then, were Louis Howe, Harry Hopkins, and Marguerite "Missy" Lehand, the president's private and confidential secretary, who had been with him since his unsuccessful vice-presidential campaign in 1920.

Mrs. Roosevelt had a problem with the cocktail hour. Prohibition was still the law of the land, and the gin and Scotch and bourbon served in the West Sitting Hall were strictly illegal. She kept her peace. Franklin Roosevelt had ignored Prohibition from the beginning. There had always been a cocktail hour. Rumor had it that most of the liquor served in the governor's mansion in Albany and now in the White House came from a Massachusetts banker named Joseph Kennedy, who apparently imported it, using fast motorboats to meet ships at sea and run the liquor to inlets on Cape Cod and Martha's Vineyard.

On this day in May, the summer's damp heat had already settled over Washington, slowing everyone down as people sweated and sat in the currents of air from electric fans. Evening brought little respite. The British

Foreign Office listed Washington as a hardship station and paid people extra to come there, as it did people sent to tropical capitals in Africa, Asia, and Latin America.

This evening only Louie, Harry, and Missy had responded to the president's cheery call of "Who's home?" The president sat in his wheelchair and happily shook martinis in his silver shaker. He had recently changed his recipe. Having for years mixed martinis with five parts of gin to one of vermouth, he was now making them stronger: seven to one. Mrs. Roosevelt had seen her formidable mother-in-law become giddy after drinking two of those.

"Will you join us, Babs?" the president asked. Babs was his nickname for Mrs. Roosevelt.

She rarely sat in on the cocktail hour. She was not skilled in the light repartee that the president so loved and that was invariably a feature of these sessions. In any case, she usually left the White House in the evening, sometimes for dinner with friends, more often to represent the president at some function it would have been burdensome for him to attend.

"I've been invited to attend a dinner of the executive board of the United Mine Workers," she said.

"I hope you're wearing chain mail under your dress," said the president.

Mrs. Roosevelt smiled weakly. This was the kind of banter she could not join. "I shall probably be late," she said.

The president poured martinis for Louie, Harry, and

Missy. Each of them would rather have drunk something else, but Franklin Roosevelt took such innocent pleasure in his martinis that they did not like to ask for the rye or bourbon they preferred.

The president raised his glass. "To happy days," he said. It was an allusion to his campaign theme song, "Happy Days Are Here Again."

At fifty-one, Franklin Roosevelt was a big, robust man—he was, that is, except for his legs, which were paralyzed and withered by polio. The president and his sons were all big men. Mrs. Roosevelt herself was well over six feet tall.

Franklin Roosevelt had a large strong head with a jutting jaw. His hair was thick and healthy, beginning to turn gray only at the sides. He had bushy eyebrows. His eyes sat within a tangle of deep lines, often obscured by his pince-nez. He smoked Camel cigarettes in a holder, which, gripped atilt in his teeth, became a Roosevelt signature. As the fashion of the time dictated, he wore double-breasted suits, often rumpled and in need of pressing.

Louis McHenry Howe was a graying, wizened gnome, sixty-two years old. He was in constant ill health, hacking and coughing incessantly. The cause of his problem was apparent to him and to everyone who knew him: he was a chain-smoker who literally did light his next Sweet Caporal cigarette from the tip of his last. His ill-fitting suits were smeared with ash. He smoked while he ate, while he drank—during whatever he was doing; and he inhaled deeply.

But he was a political genius. He was a journalist by profession. Franklin Roosevelt had come to his attention while Roosevelt was serving as a state senator in Albany. He had attached himself to FDR. It was Howe who had convinced the future president to return to politics after his polio attack cost him the use of his legs. It was Louis Howe who had convinced the at-first-reluctant Eleanor Roosevelt to become a campaigner. Now he was the president's closest adviser. He lived in a suite of rooms on the third floor of the White House, and he was always available.

Harry Hopkins—Harry the Hop to FDR, who had also given the sobriquet Missy to Marguerite LeHand—was a small man as compared to the president. He was forty-three years old and had served FDR as emergency relief administrator in Albany. He was in Washington to administer the Federal Emergency Relief program. He was already the most controversial man in the New Deal. A senator questioned emergency relief, asking if it were not true that all would work out "in the long run." Harry Hopkins's reply was quoted everywhere—"People don't eat in the long run, Senator. They must eat every day."

Marguerite Alice LeHand, Missy, was thirty-seven years old and was a handsome blonde, a Roman Catholic, originally from Massachusetts, later from New York. She was the president's confidante and adviser, not just his secretary. She called the president Effdee, meaning F.D. He dictated most of his correspondence to other secretaries, who typed the letters; but Missy read them before they went out. "This doesn't sound like you, Effdee," she would say, pointing at a passage in a letter. On one occasion she listened to him reading the draft of a speech on economics that he was to deliver before a mass audience at the Polo Grounds. The speechwriters and several cabinet officers were present. Missy began to shake her head. Finally she spoke: "By this time the bleachers will be empty, and the holders of boxes will be streaming up the aisles."

No one in the White House misunderstood Missy's relationship with the president. She met his needs. She ate with him, drank with him, joked with him. Mrs. Roosevelt admitted that she could not have functioned as she did without Missy. With no Missy she would have felt obligated to stay at home and do as much as she could to fulfill what she regarded as wifely duties. But Missy took care of those. She worked with him on his stamp collection. She arranged little surprises, such as an impromptu after-dinner poker game.

There was endless speculation as to whether or not there was an intimate physical relationship between them. No one dared confront the president with that question. It was known that during the twenties, when he spent winters cruising Florida and Caribbean waters on a boat too unglamourous to be called a yacht, swimming in the warm waters and still hoping to regain the use of his legs, Missy was with him. Mrs. Roosevelt visited the boat rarely. Cruising bored her, and she had important duties in New York City. Visitors to the boat saw Missy, in her bathing suit, sitting on Franklin's lap, with an arm draped over his shoulder. In the governor's mansion in Albany and in the White House she slept with him. No one would ever know if that was only companionable, or if it was something more. No one knew, and no one would ask.

Mrs. Roosevelt knew about all of this and did not object. She knew something else: that Missy was in love with Franklin. She doubted that his affection for Missy amounted to love.

"What's on the silver screen tonight?" the president asked Missy.

"A thriller. *Frankenstein.*"

Bell & Howell had given the president a sixteen-millimeter sound projector, and Hollywood studios sent sixteen-millimeter versions of their films to the White House. Missy had learned to thread and run the projector. They watched films often. On other nights they listened to music on his record player.

After the cocktail hour, the president retired to his bedroom suite, where his valet helped him in and out of the bathtub and into his pajamas. He propped him up on pillows on his bed. Missy went upstairs and changed into a nightgown and peignoir. They ordered dinner then, which was brought up on trays from the White House kitchen.

So—a Friday evening in the White House in mid-May 1933.

For Mrs. Roosevelt it was a very different kind of evening. In the main banquet room of the Mayflower Hotel she sat at the speakers' table on a dais. To her right was the redoubtable president of the United Mine Workers, John L. Lewis.

John Llewellyn Lewis was born the son of a Welsh coal miner in Iowa in 1880. He had left school and gone to work in the mines after completing the seventh grade. Soon he became a labor leader, and in 1920 he was elected president of the UMW. He was certainly the most flamboyant labor leader in the United States—and to many people, not just those in his union, he was the most effective.

His head was submerged under a huge shock of unruly hair. His eyebrows were immense and bushy. His frown and stare could frighten. Great jowls bordered his lower face. His lips were fleshy and flexible, and from between them rumbled a deep, expressive, not unmusical voice that he used to excoriate the mine owners and their political allies with allusions to ancient and modern literature and epithets of his own invention.

He was much quoted. Being criticized for taking too much credit for improvements in mine safety, he said, "He who tooteth not his own horn, the same shall not *beee* tooted."

He talked animatedly with Mrs. Roosevelt during the dinner.

"I am sorry, my dear lady, that you will not essay some of this excellent bourbon."

Mrs. Roosevelt smiled. "I wonder, Mr. Lewis, if it would be entirely appropriate for the wife of the president of the United States to be seen drinking what remains illegal."

Lewis half smiled, half frowned, and said, "Napoleon said something like this—'I am not an ordinary man, and the laws that govern ordinary men do not govern me.' If Frank could be here, he would enjoy this good bourbon."

"Franklin is not an ordinary man," she said. "I am afraid I am rather an ordinary woman."

"Not at all, my dear lady. Not at all."

The fact was, Mrs. Roosevelt had a reputation throughout the country for being a not-very-attractive, awkward, and gawky woman—and this from people who were not obsessed with hating all things Roosevelt.

She had two large protruding teeth, but they did not spoil her face. When she did not smile too broadly, they were out of sight.

She was not entirely without fault in the matter of her appearance. For some reason she had utterly excruciating taste in clothes. It was a time of unflattering styles, but she seemed to have a talent for choosing the most unflattering things she could find—dresses with excessive numbers of buttons, inappropriate frills, floppy collars . . . hats with gaudy feathers and useless veils, and so on. When she dressed simply, she was a comely woman, tall and slender. And she could be poised.

Her inaugural gown was simple and stylish. As though she were aware that it flattered her, she was poised and confident in it and sat for a charming photo portrait. Mornings she liked to ride horseback in Rock Creek Park with her friend Elinor Morgenthau, Hudson Valley neighbor and wife of FDR's soon-to-be secretary of the treasury. When she rode, she wore simple riding clothes: jodhpurs, a plain jacket over a blouse, and a wide yellow ribbon to hold her hair in place. In those togs she was attractive indeed.

Tonight, unhappily, she was wearing a dark-blue dress with a row of white buttons from her collar down to the hem of her skirt. In that, with her feathered hat—one plain long feather sweeping from side to side—she really did look gawky.

"I am quite curious, Mr. Lewis, as to why there are no more Negro miners."

"Maybe because they've got better sense than to go down in the mines," he said.

"But I have been told," she went on, "that some of your miners will not allow a Negro man to join the union."

"It's dangerous work, Mrs. Roosevelt. It depends on faithful teamwork. Many of the miners feel they don't want to trust their lives to Negroes."

"But surely—"

"You are interested in social justice," he interrupted. "Well, so am I. But right now my attention has to be centered on keeping miners alive. In a perfect world, men would not be sent down into unsafe mines. The government would insist on mine safety. When we come nearer to that perfect world, I will look into the question of whether or not some mines might be worked by Negro crews."

"Should they not work side by side with the white miners?"

Lewis shook his head so vigorously that his jowls flopped. "That would be asking too much," he said.

"I have brief remarks prepared. I suppose it would be well if I don't mention this issue."

"I suggest you don't. This kind of change is not going to come to pass this year or next year or the year after. *Festina lente.*"

Mrs. Roosevelt had a classical education and knew what he meant—"Make haste slowly."

As Mrs. Roosevelt was being driven back to the White House, a rainstorm broke over Washington. Blue and red lightning flashed in clouds briefly made visible. Rain fell in sheets. Her driver had to slow to a crawl because his headlights could not entirely penetrate the sweeping raindrops.

The rain inconvenienced but few Washingtonians. A

small crowd sheltered in the foyer of the Gayety Burlesque, where a show had just ended. Others huddled in the doorways of bars. Otherwise, very few were out.

Washington was not a late-night town. A desk sergeant at police headquarters, filling out an arrest report, would ask, "Clerk or mechanic?" To his mind, there were just two kinds of people: those who worked with paper and those who worked with tools; and in Washington in 1933 he was not far from right.

Washington was a Southern town. It was rigidly segregated. Segregation was not a way of life; it was a self-defense. No matter how lowly the station a man held in life, if he was white, he was the superior of every Negro. This was understood. It was not a debatable proposition.

The *old* Washingtonians, those who could claim their families had owned the land on which the city was built, segregated themselves in another way. They kept to their homes and clubs and did not mingle with the clerks and mechanics. They lived in musty mansions, all with the same cloying odor of old dust and burning incense, in the midst of priceless antiques; and they invited each other for visits—and few others. Even so sedate a magazine as the *Saturday Evening Post* called them "cave dwellers."

They had invited the Hoovers occasionally, though Hoover was an Iowan and an engineer. They had invited the Coolidges, even though Coolidge was originally a small-town Massachusetts lawyer. The Hardings, never—not those gaudy-rude, style-ignorant, hard-drinking bumpkins. They had been pleased with the election of

FDR, though none of them would have voted for him, even if Washingtonians had had the vote. At least Franklin, of the Hyde Park Roosevelts, and Eleanor, of the Oyster Bay Roosevelts, were to the manner born and could be expected to conduct themselves as aristocrats. The cave dwellers had not yet decided that Franklin was a traitor to his class and that Eleanor was a protocommunist.

The New Dealers imported into Washington by the new president were shocking people. They might know the price of eggs in China, but they knew nothing of how to dress and act. They never wore evening clothes—probably didn't own any—and appeared at formal dinners in dark business suits at best, baggy tweeds more likely, smoking cheap tobacco in curved pipes that slurped when they drew, from want of cleaning. Shortly, their kind was excluded from polite society—the cave dwellers telling themselves they had *tried* to accommodate these professors of economics and such ilk but had been accorded no respect by them.

Mrs. Roosevelt had come to feel isolated in Washington. More and more, she found solace in her own cherished friendships, and she went back to New York to embrace them as often as she could.

Washington was an idiosyncratic, alien city. She had not wanted to be First Lady. She did her best to adjust.

II

1

RETURNING TO THE WHITE House, the car carrying the First Lady was waved past the guardhouse on Pennsylvania Avenue, so the driver could take her to the North Portico, where she could enter without having to walk even a few steps in the rain.

As she often did, Mrs. Roosevelt climbed the East Stairs to the second floor, rather than using one of the elevators. Though the president had to use the elevators, Mrs. Roosevelt knew they were old and cranky, and she had a vision of herself stuck between floors. Others had been stuck. Why should she be exempt? One of her nightmares was the utter panic that would ensue if the president, in his wheelchair, were to get stuck in the West Elevator.

The White House was patrolled night and day by uniformed members of the White House police and by plainclothes agents of the Secret Service. Gone was the day, as in the time of Abraham Lincoln, when anyone could wander in off the street and amble through the building, visiting any room he saw fit. Security was loose, as the experience of later years would dramatically demonstrate, but there *were* personnel on duty. Visitors were conducted where they were supposed to go. Strangers were stopped at the door.

Reaching the top of the stairs, Mrs. Roosevelt turned right, entered the Center Hall, and abruptly encountered a tight knot of hushed men, kneeling over and standing above a prone figure on the floor.

One of them broke away and hurried to her. "I'm sorry, Ma'am," he said, "but I have to suggest you go back downstairs and come up on the West Stairs or in the West Elevator." He nodded toward the figure on the floor. "There is something there that you shouldn't see."

She frowned and stared. "A dead body," she said. "Bloody, too. What happened?"

"I am afraid he was murdered, Ma'am."

"Who is . . . was he?"

"His name is . . . Well, it's a little strange. His name is Douglas Douglas. He was a member of the uniformed White House police."

"And he was murdered right there? I mean, he was murdered within a few feet of the door to the president's bedroom?"

"Yes, Ma'am. Now let me take you around to—"

"I have seen dead bodies before, Mr. . . . Haven't we met?"

"Yes, Ma'am. I'm Stanlislaw Szczygiel, of the Secret Service."

"Of course."

She did remember Stanlislaw Szczygiel. Fortunately his name was pronounced "Seagull." He was fifty-nine years old, and he had begun his White House career under President William McKinley. He was a squat, square man, both of face and physique; and perhaps his most memorable feature was his oversized, gin-reddened nose. He was dressed in a dark-brown double-breasted suit that made him look all the wider.

"How did he die, Mr. Szczygiel?"

"By knife, Ma'am. Knifed in the belly, several times."

"Wasn't he carrying a pistol?"

Szczygiel nodded. "He didn't pull the pistol. Pain and shock may explain that." He shrugged. "I wish I knew why he didn't pull it. He was well trained with it."

"Have you any idea who killed him?"

"No, Ma'am."

"Am I then to understand we have a murder mystery in the White House?"

"I'm afraid we do."

"You will investigate."

"We will, Ma'am, thoroughly. But—"

"But . . . ?"

"Well, you see, investigation is not our forte. We are not trained to investigate. The Secret Service is in the business of protection. So is the White House police."

"Then who?"

Szczygiel glanced around as if concerned that he might be overheard. "Technically, I suppose it should be the FBI."

"That seems to distress you, Mr. Szczygiel."

He glanced around again. "Yes, Ma'am," he said in a low voice. "You see . . . I imagine the president will want this matter subjected to as little press attention as possible. Mr. J. Edgar Hoover will want *as much* press attention as possible . . . provided it is favorable to him. He is a . . . publicity hound, Mrs. Roosevelt."

She smiled. " 'He who tooteth not his own horn, the same shall not *be* tooted.' "

Szczygiel, too, smiled. "I know the quotation."

"Have we any alternative? Is there any precedent?"

"Yes, Ma'am. A housemaid, a Negro girl, was stabbed to death by her boyfriend, in the White House, during the administration of William Howard Taft. We asked the District police to investigate. They did and shortly arrested her boyfriend. He was hanged about five weeks later. Of course . . . in those days there was no FBI. But we recognized that the District police had a Homicide Division with experience and expertise investigating murders. What was more, they were *circumspect.* They were quite circumspect. The press never learned that the murder had happened inside the White House."

"Mr. Szczygiel, be so kind as to call the D.C. police and ask for assistance in a highly confidential matter."

"Yes, Ma'am."

Mrs. Roosevelt went to the door of the president's bedroom and knocked gently.

Missy appeared, wearing peignoir and nightgown. In the bedroom, the projector was still running, and a film was flickering on the screen. Apparently the president had decided he wanted to view a second picture from his small library.

Mrs. Roosevelt put a finger to her mouth. "Missy," she said in a very low voice, "one of the White House policemen has just been murdered, right here in the hall, only a few feet from this door. Don't tell the president until his film is finished. Then tell him the matter is being handled discreetly and that he need not worry about it."

Missy stuck her head out and saw the bloody corpse. *"Oh, my God!"* she whispered.

"There is nothing the president can do tonight. The guard here will be . . . I should think tripled. Tell him I will come to him in the morning to tell him all I know."

2

THE MAN FROM D.C. police headquarters arrived some thirty minutes later.

"I'm sorry to be so long," he said. "They reached me at home. I was in bed."

"Murderers don't often consider our convenience," said Szczygiel dryly.

"No. But it would have been the first full night's sleep I've had in two weeks."

"We are sorry," said Mrs. Roosevelt.

"Thank you, Ma'am. I'm Lieutenant Edward Kennelly, homicide detail. I've never been in the White House before and have never met a First Lady. I wish it could have been in happier circumstances."

Licutenant Kennelly was the apotheosis of an Irish cop: bulky, white-haired, blue-eyed, ruddy. He looked as though he could have picked up Stanislaw Szczygiel and thrown him down the stairs.

Kennelly squatted by the body and stared at it. "When did this happen?" he asked.

"About an hour ago," said Szczygiel. "A maid found him. The president had ordered coffee and brandy from the kitchen. When she came up, she found him. I don't think he could have been lying there more than ten minutes. These halls are patrolled. That's the door to the president's bedroom."

"His jacket and shirt are open," said Kennelly.

"We called a doctor up from the White House physician's office. A navy lieutenant was on duty at this hour."

Kennelly lifted the bloody jacket. "Stabbed right through," he said.

"Six times," said Szczygiel.

"And the man was carrying a gun."

"We guessed the shock of the first wound probably immobilized him."

"Still . . . The man had to *approach* him. He had to get

damned close before he pulled the knife. Uh—Which could mean the victim knew the man. Maybe he wasn't on his guard, because he didn't expect any trouble from that source. When a man with a knife kills a man with a gun, it makes for an interesting case, doesn't it?"

A captain of the uniformed police spoke. "Can the body be removed now?" he asked.

"Yes, it can," said Lieutenant Kennelly. "Take it for an autopsy."

"Has his family been notified?" asked Mrs. Roosevelt.

"Yes," said the captain. "He had a wife and two small children, a boy and a girl. We sent a man to notify them. He picked up their priest on the way."

Mrs. Roosevelt drew a deep breath and shook her head.

"We will have half a dozen men on the second floor all night," said the captain.

"Together with three or four of ours, of the Secret Service," said Szczygiel.

"You are thinking what I am thinking," said Mrs. Roosevelt grimly.

"Yes," said Szczygiel. "Douglas Douglas may have been killed by a man who came here to attempt to murder the president."

3

MRS. ROOSEVELT LOOKED AT Szczygiel and Kennelly. "Gentlemen," she said, "I think we might retire to a private room and talk."

She led them east, through the wide doors that separated the Center Hall and West Sitting Hall from the Stair Hall and East Hall, then right into the short passage into the Lincoln Sitting Room. She switched on lights.

"Since you've never been in the White House before, Lieutenant Kennelly, you might like to have a quick look at the famous Lincoln Bedroom."

The bedroom was dominated by an elaborately carved rosewood bed. The bed, sofa, chairs, and desk were all mid–nineteenth century in style: heavy and gloomy.

"Contrary to what many people think," said Mrs. Roosevelt, "President Lincoln never slept in this room, and he never slept in that bed. This room was his office. He signed the Emancipation Proclamation here. The room was made a bedroom and guest room only some years later."

The Lincoln Sitting Room was much smaller. Bedroom, sitting room, and bathroom, it constituted a suite for visitors to the White House. Because it was so gloomy, most visitors preferred the light and airy suite across the hall.

They sat down in the Lincoln Sitting Room, and Mrs. Roosevelt picked up the telephone and ordered coffee and small pastries brought up from the kitchen.

"What, if anything, can we assume?" she asked. "For example, do we know how the man got in here? Do we know how he got out? Or even that he did get out?"

"We've checked on that," said Szczygiel. "No one left the White House through the gates after about nine o'clock—no one, that is, except Negro employees of the usher's office and the kitchen, all of whom were well known to the gate guards.

"Entry? No one came in—again excepting staff coming in for late-night work. The kitchen is open all night, as you know. The usher can send messengers or errand-runners at any hour."

"The West Wing?" she asked. She was referring to the separate wing where the executive offices were located, including the president's famous Oval Office.

"To enter the main house from the West Wing you have to pass a guard station. No one did. No one left the house from the West Wing either."

"Then . . . ?"

Szczygiel shrugged. "I am afraid we have to accept the fact that the White House is not a secure building. There are several ways to get in and out, if you know the White House intimately."

"And to walk past the policemen and Secret Service agents?" Kennelly asked.

"We've already questioned security staff," said Szczygiel. "No one noticed anyone unusual."

Kennelly shook his head.

"Am I to understand, then, that an intruder can reach

the very door of the president's bedroom without being detected or stopped?"

"We do the best we can," Szczygiel said weakly.

"And Officer Douglas Douglas *just happened* to be there?"

"No. It was his beat. He was supposed to be there. Or somewhere near, not out of sight of the president's door."

"And this one officer," said Kennelly, "was killed. If the man had come to attack the president, why didn't he go in? He had killed the only man who stood between him and the president's door."

"I can think of a reason," said Mrs. Roosevelt. "This may be fanciful, but—well . . . When you went near the door, you could hear the sound of voices inside. I myself, when I went to tell Missy, heard muffled voices. It was the sound of voices coming from the movie projector. The president watched a movie tonight, maybe two of them. Part of the time . . . dialog. The would-be assassin—if that is what he was—may have supposed two or three men were with the president." She shrugged. "Absurd, I know, but maybe—"

Kennelly shook his head. "Not absurd. Not fanciful. Unlikely maybe, but cases often turn on such unlikely explanations."

"Douglas was armed with his service revolver," said Szczygiel. "I can't imagine why he didn't pull it, unless he knew the man and saw no danger."

"Who would want to kill President Roosevelt? And why?" Kennelly asked.

"Booth thought he had his reasons," said Szczygiel. "Guiteau, who killed President Garfield, was just a nut. So was Czolgosz, who killed President McKinley. And Zangara, who meant to kill President-elect Roosevelt and instead killed Mayor Cermak, was a nut. Some people don't have to have reasons, not in the way you and I think of reasons. Some people can't even pretend to be rational."

An attempt on FDR's life had been made in Miami on February 15. The Twentieth Amendment not yet having taken effect, the inauguration would not occur until March 4, and on February 15 Franklin Roosevelt was still president-elect. He had just come ashore from a vacation cruise and was riding in an open car through Bayfront Park. With him in the car was Mayor Anton Cermak of Chicago. Suddenly five shots were fired. The president-elect was not hit, but Mayor Cermak was fatally wounded. He died on March 6.

The shooter was Giuseppe Zangara, a thirty-two-year-old unemployed bricklayer from Paterson, New Jersey. His motive was that he hated all presidents. Mayor Cermak died on March 6. Zangara was indicted for murder that same day. He pleaded guilty, and two weeks later he was electrocuted in the Florida electric chair, "Old Sparky." Just before he was put to death, he complained bitterly that the "filthy capitalists" did not allow his execution to be photographed.

"People without rational motives are the most difficult to identify," said Kennelly. "They make for the most difficult cases."

"It would seem," said Mrs. Roosevelt, "that this crime was planned for some time."

"All of the assassinations have been," said Szczygiel. "All of the *attempted* assassinations, too."

"Can we summarize?" asked Mrs. Roosevelt. "What do we know? We know that a man with a knife came to the door of the president's bedroom. We know that he was confronted by Officer Douglas Douglas. We know that he killed Officer Douglas with a knife. Those are the only firm facts we have, are they not?"

"Those facts clearly imply some things," said Kennelly. "For example, they imply that the killer knew the White House and its routines sufficiently well that he was able to move from wherever he entered to the door of the president's bedroom without being stopped. That suggests a member of the White House staff, doesn't it?"

"Yes, but not necessarily a staffer of this administration," said Mrs. Roosevelt.

"He seems to have known how to get into the White House surreptitiously," said Szczygiel.

"How could he do that?" asked Mrs. Roosevelt.

"Well, there's an underground passage between the east end of the first floor and the Treasury Building. The president himself sometimes uses it when he wants to leave the White House without being noticed. He goes up to the first floor on an elevator, and his car is waiting for him at the rear of the building, on Fifteenth Street. It is closed by a steel gate, locked with a padlock. A skilled man could pick that old-fashionedy padlock. Or, I suppose he could some way get a key."

"Which would bring him into the east end of the house," said Kennelly. "And from there?"

"He could climb the stairs. Being careful, he could avoid the security personnel."

"He could have taken Elevator Number One all the way to the third floor," said Mrs. Roosevelt, "then worked his way down from there."

"Yes," said Szczygiel. "Security men would have noticed the elevator going up, but when it did not stop at their floor, they would have let it become the worry of the men on the next floor up."

"And there are few if any security personnel on the third floor," said Mrs. Roosevelt.

"What's up there?" asked Kennelly.

"Storage, chiefly," said Szczygiel. "Linen is stored in one room. There's a cedar room to discourage moths in blankets and so on. Books are stored up there. And files. Besides that, there are several bedrooms, some of them in suites with sitting rooms and bathrooms. Mr. Howe has a suite up there. So does Miss LeHand, the president's secretary. Mr. Hopkins sometimes stays up there.

"Those suites are not as grand as those on the second floor, but they are comfortable."

They were interrupted as the coffee and pastries Mrs. Roosevelt had ordered were delivered. It was her judgment that Szczygiel and Kennelly would rather have had whiskey or gin, but she was not prepared to offer those just now.

"I suppose there are people who would like to kill the president," said Kennelly. "I mean, aside from nuts. Forgive me, Ma'am, but Mr. Roosevelt is one of the best beloved and most thoroughly hated men in the United States."

"There are many," she said, "who dislike accepting the verdict of an election. They think they know better than the voters."

"But would they go so far as to try to assassinate the president?" Szczygiel asked.

"Yes, assuredly," said Mrs. Roosevelt. "When you are convinced of your infallibility, nothing much is beyond you."

"We are making an assumption here," said Kennelly. "It is a reasonable assumption, but—The man who killed Officer Douglas may have come to the White House to kill Officer Douglas. Or for some other reason. Maybe he came to steal something and just happened to be caught where he was. I'll work on the premise that he was here to attempt to assassinate the president, but I think we should not exclude other possibilities."

Mrs. Roosevelt nodded. "Well said."

4

ON HER WAY ALONG the halls to her bedroom, Mrs. Roosevelt assured herself that the presidential suite was now well guarded. The police captain saluted her and swept his arm around at the four men on duty in the Center Hall.

From her bedroom window she could see rain still falling on the Ellipse. She realized suddenly that she was very tired—yet so tense she knew she would have difficulty falling asleep. She decided to soak for a while in a hot bath.

In hot, soapy water she relaxed gradually. Her mind ran over the months they had lived in the White House. The new administration was in the midst of what would come to be called the Hundred Days. They might have been called the Heady Days.

On March 6 the president had issued an executive order closing all banks for four days. The idea was to stop the runs on the banks. On March 9 the Congress passed the Emergency Banking Act, confirming what the president had done. Possession of gold was made a crime. All gold had to be turned in at banks.

The Agricultural Adjustment Act, among other things, authorized payment of subsidies to farmers who agreed to reduce their production of certain commodities.

The Civilian Conservation Corps, or CCC, was established. Unemployed young men could move into camps and be employed in forestry and the improvement of national parks. This took many thousands of young men off the streets and into useful employment, for which they were paid thirty dollars a month.

On April 19, the president issued an executive order banning the exportation of gold, which meant that foreign creditors would have to accept payment in the U.S. dollar, which would fluctuate in value and find its place among the other devalued currencies of the world.

The Tennessee Valley Authority Act authorized the federal government to take over and operate a huge hydroelectric dam complex that had been built at government expense during the World War—also to build more dams and power plants.

Steps were taken to regulate the sale of securities, specifically requiring issuers of stocks and bonds to disclose all relevant information—subject to heavy penalties.

And there was more. No wonder some people might want to kill Franklin D. Roosevelt.

Now this. Now tonight.

Lieutenant Kennelly was right in thinking that the killing in the Center Hall may not have been an element of an attempt to assassinate the president. But it certainly had the look of it.

She resolved to keep close track of the investigation.

Finally she felt herself relax and become sleepy. She pulled the stopper and let the water run out, lest she go to sleep in the tub, submerge, and come up spluttering.

Looking out the window one final time, she saw the rain still falling. Somehow it was restful.

III

1

SATURDAY MORNING DAWNED SUNNY and green in Washington. Mrs. Roosevelt was up early, as she always was. She had herself driven to the stable in Rock Creek Park, where she had her horse saddled. Elinor Morgenthau, who was a pretty, petite, dark-haired woman, appeared shortly, and the two women mounted their horses and began their morning ride.

Although the rain had stopped sometime after midnight and before dawn, water still dripped from the trees and spotted their riding clothes. Even so, cantering along the bridle paths was exhilarating.

Mrs. Roosevelt knew that the president would not be up much before eight, and she expected to be back in the White House by then, at which time she would see him and report what she knew about the death of Officer Douglas Douglas.

Which wasn't much. She expected to learn more from

later meetings with Agent Szczygiel and Lieutenant Kennelly.

"Have you heard what Will Rogers said about the ease with which Frank has gotten his program through Congress?" Mrs. Morgenthau asked.

"What did he say?"

"He said Congress would applaud if the president burned down the Capitol Building. 'Well, anyhow, he knows how to start a fire.' "

Mrs. Roosevelt could laugh at that. All too many of the jokes circulating about the Roosevelts were cruel.

"Henry thinks we should have a new car. I wonder. He wants to buy a Packard, which is about the most expensive car on the road. He's willing to pay more than two thousand dollars for it!

"He could get a perfectly good Pontiac or Dodge for less than six hundred."

Mrs. Roosevelt nodded. "I'm interested in the new Ford V Eight."

Elinor Morgenthau always tried to find something amusing to tell, like the Will Rogers comment. She said now—

"I have been more than amused by the exchange between the makers of Luckies and the makers of Camels. You notice that Lucky advertises, 'It's toasted.' Well, Camel has a huge sign up in Times Square that says, 'CAMEL. Never parched or toasted.' "

"That's like the advertising for canned tuna fish," said Mrs. Roosevelt. "People were accustomed to canned salmon, which is naturally pinkish or red. Opening a can of tuna, they found this unpalatable-looking pale fish meat that did not appeal to them. So the tuna packers advertised, 'Guaranteed not to turn red in the can.' "

"Walter Winchell advertises Lucky Strike cigarettes," said Elinor. "He says he's smoked them for eleven years. I wouldn't believe that abhorrent liar if he said he smoked dog doo."

"Nor would I. But he has a huge following."

"The Chicago World's Fair will open in a couple of weeks," said Elinor. "I understand that Sally Rand will dance there, in the nude."

"That will guarantee large attendance," said Mrs. Roosevelt. "I wish I could see it."

"You approve?"

The First Lady shrugged. "I try not to be judgmental," she said.

2

THE PRESIDENT BELIEVED IN a hearty breakfast: eggs, bacon, toast, marmalade, and coffee. It was brought up from the White House kitchen on a bed tray, and he sat up in bed and read newspapers as he ate. The president loved dogs, and the first Roosevelt White House dog was usually brought to his bedroom for a morning visit and for nibbles handed her by the president from his breakfast. This dog was named Maggie. Maggie did not scamper around the room, leaping on and off the bed, but sat contentedly, usually with her head tipped a little to one side, making small sounds to remind her master that she was there and would love another bite of toast or a bit of bacon.

Mrs. Roosevelt came in, still in her riding clothes. Usually she did not let Franklin see her in her riding clothes. They constituted, she supposed, a painful reminder of what he could no longer do. Before his polio, he had been a very active man, interested in all sports. He'd had an ice boat, and on cold winter mornings when the Hudson was frozen over, he had sped over the ice, driven by the wind in the boat's tall sail—a reckless sport, his wife and mother agreed.

"Well, Babs. Have a pleasant ride?"

"Yes, indeed."

"There is nothing in the morning papers about a man being murdered in the White House last night."

She sat down in a chair facing his bed. "With good fortune there won't be," she said.

"Amen to that. But how is that going to be arranged?"

"By keeping Mr. Hoover out of the investigation. I took the liberty last night of asking a District homicide detective to conduct the investigation. There is precedent for it. The District police investigated a murder in the White House during the Taft presidency. They were most circumspect, and the newspapers never reported that a murder had happened within the precincts of the White House."

"How do you know?"

"Agent Szczygiel told me. Stanislaw Szczygiel has been with the Secret Service since the days of William McKinley."

"The Secret Service could not—?"

"No. They are specialists in protection, not investigation."

"Of course."

"The man from the homicide squad seems quite competent. His name is Lieutenant Edward Kennelly."

"I suppose you think the murderer is a would-be presidential assassin."

"Tentatively, yes, we do think so."

"*We* think so? Are you sticking your nib in this, Babs?"

"A little," she said. "Only a little. Someone must represent the interests of the president—"

"The presidency."

"The presidency," she agreed. "And I don't see how *you* can be that representative."

"Well . . . So far you've done well to keep John Edgar Hoover out of it. The man is a publicity hound and an empire builder."

"There is a rumor as well that he is secretly an ardent sodomite," she said. "It is whispered that he is 'married' to his assistant, Clyde Tolson."

"I don't like that," said the president, "but I can't fire him on that rumor. In fact, I suppose it wouldn't hamper his conducting an effective investigation. It would be his trumpeting the case and claiming credit for any results he achieved that would be intolerable."

"Intolerable," she agreed.

"On the other hand, Babs, you must not meddle in this matter. If it should become public and become known that you had butted in, the furor would also be intolerable. You are not Hawkshaw."

She smiled at the reference. Hawkshaw was a comic-strip detective, very loosely modeled on Sherlock Holmes.

"Alright?" he asked.

"I shut out Mr. Hoover to be circumspect," she said. "I would defeat my own purpose if I were noncircumspect myself."

3

ED KENNELLY ARRIVED AT the White House about ten o'clock. Stan Szczygiel led him to a room on the ground floor, where both men changed into blue denim coveralls and rubber boots. Stan provided long, powerful flashlights. Kennelly shoved his thirty-eight-caliber Colt service revolver into a deep pocket. Stan carried a crowbar.

"Now," said Stan, "I'm going to show you something about the White House."

The White House kitchen was an old-fashioned facility with a huge range recently converted to burn gas instead of wood or coal, white-enamel sinks, cabinets, and in the center an enormous table for cutting meat and vegetables, rolling dough, and whatever. To the right a door opened onto a medium-sized room called the refrigerator room. The temperature in there was maintained at a constant thirty-five degrees.

Szczygiel shoved aside several cartons and uncovered a steel manhole cover. He used his crowbar to pry up the manhole cover, used his flashlight to illuminate the vertical shaft underneath, and gestured to Ed that he should go down first.

When Ed hesitated, Stan said, "Somebody has got to replace the cover."

The shaft was lined with old, worn bricks, and steel cleats set in the wall formed a ladder. Kennelly descended some twelve feet, Stan following as soon as he had pulled the manhole cover back into place.

The shaft ended four feet or so short of the bottom of a horizontal tunnel that ran away in the darkness in both directions. Roughly a foot of water stood in the tunnel, and the walls were dripping wet.

"See what it is?" asked Stan.

"I'd guess a rainwater drain," said Ed

"Exactly. Last night this tunnel was *full* of water. Last night we'd have *drowned* in here."

Kennelly aimed his flashlight first one way and then the other, probing as far as its beam would reach in the black darkness.

"Let's go this way first," said Szczygiel, pointing east.

As they crouched and worked their way, they came on interceptor tunnels: smaller tunnels that carried water from the roof drains into this one. Orienting himself as best he could, Ed judged this tunnel was under the north side of the White House.

"When was this tunnel built?" he asked Szczygiel.

"When the house was built," said Stan.

"Where does it go, ultimately?"

"Originally it went into a creek that ran very near, called Tiber Creek, later called Goose Creek. Decades later it was joined to one of the main Washington drainage tunnels. Goose Creek ran into what is now the Tidal Basin. The city tunnel ran into that water. The first flush toilets in the White House discharged into this tunnel and the other one on the south side. Today, nothing but rainwater is allowed to run into the Tidal Basin."

"Must have been a mess," said Ed.

"Odors from the tunnels leaked up into the house. People prayed for rain. When it did rain, it flushed out the tunnels. The water runs through here in a torrent."

They reached another vertical shaft.

"It comes out in what we now call the Library. The manhole cover is under the carpet. I doubt our friend came up that way. The tunnel over here connects to the parallel tunnel under the south side of the house. Manholes over there open on what is called the Gold Room and on the White House physician's office. Our friend could have crawled through the connecting tunnel and come up in the Gold Room."

"He'd have had to have stashed clothes somewhere," said Kennelly.

"If he knew enough to use these tunnels, he knew enough to find a place to stash clothes."

Ed stood in the shaft leading up to the Library, glad to have the chance to stand erect.

"Want to see where it goes in the other direction?" asked Stan.

"Couldn't you just tell me?"

"I'll show you," said Szczygiel.

They crept through the tunnel, shortly reaching the shaft to the refrigerator room, where they had entered. Moving on, they came to a part of the tunnel that was obviously of later construction.

"They broke into the tunnel when they were putting down the foundation for the West Wing," said Stan. "It had to be rebuilt. Otherwise, where was the rainwater going?"

Going on through, they reached old construction again. Now they moved a long distance. Reaching a vertical shaft, Stan explained that it opened into the ground floor of the State Department Building—"Which is another place where a knowledgeable man could have entered the tunnel."

They reached the end, where another vertical shaft rose. Stan shoved up the cover, and bright sunlight entered. Stan climbed out. Ed followed, relieved once more to be able to stand, relieved to be out of the dank underground. They were on the sidewalk on 17th Street, in front of the State Department Building.

Stan replaced the cover. "I suggest we walk back," he said. "No point in going back underground. But, you see, a man who knew about this could get into the White House without going through any door, without going past any guard desk."

"Well, why the hell don't—?"

"Money, my friend," said Stan. "Why don't we install barred gates and good locks at intervals in the tunnels? Money. It would require an appropriation. In the meantime, the White House is a sieve."

"For someone who knows how to get in and out," said Kennelly. "That's the key. How many people know about these tunnels?"

Szczygiel shrugged.

"You could at least weld the manhole covers shut."

"Suppose someone is down in a tunnel, not realizing it has started to rain. He could drown and be swept all the way out into the Tidal Basin. I wouldn't want to be the man who ordered that."

"Well . . . It's not my job to reform White House security," said Kennelly. "My job is to help you find out who killed Officer Douglas Douglas. This excursion through the tunnels has been helpful."

"There are others," said Szczygiel.

4

THE PRESIDENT WHEELED HIMSELF from his bedroom to the West Elevator, rode it down to the ground floor, then wheeled himself along the colonnade and into the West Wing. Bells sounded ahead of him, warning staff that the chief was on his way to the Oval Office.

He moved fast. In the colonnade between the house and the wing, he overtook a young man walking along.

"Oh. Good morning, Mr. President."

"Good morning, Brother Hay," said the president cheerfully.

Ben Hay was a young lawyer from New York, appointed by Secretary of the Interior Harold Ickes but detached from the Department of the Interior temporarily to work in the Executive Wing, where he was one of the lawyers involved in drafting legislation.

"Fine morning, Mr. President."

"It is indeed."

Hay lengthened his stride, and the president slowed down a little, and they reached the Executive Wing together.

Inside the Oval Office, he aligned his wheelchair by his desk chair and with a grunting effort of his powerful arms and shoulders transferred his body into the desk chair. The wheelchair was specially made of wood and steel, to be sturdy and yet light in weight. Shoved aside, it would not be taken out of the Oval Office but kept out of sight until the president needed it again.

The president lifted each leg with his hands and rested his feet on a box that remained always hidden under his desk. He lighted a cigarette: a Camel.

Missy came in. "Your first appointment is with the secretary of state," she said.

Secretary of State Cordell Hull was a Tennessean. He had served several terms in the House of Representatives before being elected to the Senate. He had resigned from the Senate to accept President Roosevelt's appointment as secretary of state. Soft-spoken and courtly, he was handsome, with a strong square face and white hair.

He and the president exchanged greetings, then Hull sat down across the desk from the president and came immediately to his business.

"I've had several messages from Ambassador Henderson, in Berlin," he said. "The new German government is doing some very distressing things."

"Anything I'm not aware of?" the president asked.

"Maybe. We have been aware all along that Herr Hitler and his ministers are obsessively anti-Semitic. German Jews have been harassed mercilessly. Their stores are boycotted, their customers threatened with reprisal if they continue to buy there. Their property is being confiscated. And—"

"I know," said the president.

Hull opened his briefcase. "Here is a photograph that came in the diplomatic pouch."

The president looked at the picture. It was of a grim-faced young woman put on display on a street by five

Nazi storm troopers. She was stripped to her underwear, though, as if stolidly, she still wore a straw hat decorated with artificial flowers. Suspended from a string around her neck was a placard that read—

Ich bin am Ort
das grosste Schwein
und lass mich nur
mit Juden ein!

The president's German was not strong, but he roughly translated the words to mean—

I am in this place
the grossest swine
I lie down with Jews
And only Jews!

The president shook his head and handed the photo back to Hull. "We can't break diplomatic relations over that," he said.

"This is nothing compared to what else is going on," said Hull. "As soon as the Nazis came to power, they imprisoned most of their political opponents. They established *Konzentrationslagern,* concentration camps. Conditions in them are horrible. Prisoners are overworked and underfed and subjected to sadism by their bully-boy guards. Lately they've been rounding up Jews and herding them into the camps."

The president shook his head. "That's a new one for me, though I would find it difficult to disbelieve anything of which Herr Hitler is accused."

"Tens of thousands," said Hull. "They are not even *charged* with any crime. A woman managed to get word to Ambassador Henderson that her eighteen-year-old daughter has been arrested and sent to a camp. Why? Because the commandant saw her on the street and decided he wanted her. She's his mistress now. If she wants to eat, she—Well . . . That's what's going on."

"It's distressing," said the president. "I imagine some people think we should do something about it. I should be grateful if they would suggest what."

"Whatever it would be, it would have to be economic," said Hull. "We are in no position to try to impose our will."

"And economic sanctions would run up against loud opposition in this country," said President Roosevelt. "Colonel Bertie McCormick and his *Chicago Tribune*. The isolationists . . ."

"The anti-Semites," said the secretary of state.

"Well . . . They're rather quiet," said the president. "Embarrassed."

"Do you think so? Have you seen an issue of Henry Ford's Dearborn newspaper lately? Have you seen his book? It's in four volumes and is titled *The International Jew: The World's Foremost Problem*. I don't know how much of it he actually wrote, but he publishes it, and you can find a set in any Ford agency."

"Serious stuff?"

"I haven't read it, but I assigned a man to read it. Turgid stuff, he says. He supplied me with some quotes." Hull reached into his briefcase. "Here are two passages—"

> The Jewish Question is not the number of Jews who reside here, not in the American's jealousy of the Jew's success; it is in something else, and that something else is the fact of Jewish influence on the life of the country where Jews dwell; in the United States it is the Jewish influence on American life.

> With the required manipulation of the money and food markets, enough pressure could be brought to bear on the ultimate consumers to give point to the idea of "get" . . . the idea of "get" instead of "make."

"He claims the Jews have taken over the colleges, the churches, the labor unions, and the government. Ford is a great hero in Germany. Some years ago the *Berliner Tageblatt* published a report saying he was financing Hitler and the Nazi party. I doubt that's true, but—"

"He'll go into shrieking hysterics if he gets it in his mind we are trying to do something to save the Jews from Hitler's excesses."

"He won't be the only one," said Hull.

FDR shook his head sadly. "I've got as much on my

plate as I can possibly cope with. Much as I would like to help the Jews, I don't see what I can do. It would have to be a major effort, which would meet major opposition. I don't see what I can do."

5

STAN SZCZYGIEL CAME TO the First Lady's office late in the morning.

"I have a bit of information," he said. "It seems that someone slept in one of the spare bedrooms on the third floor last night—someone unauthorized, that is."

"How do you know?" asked Mrs. Roosevelt.

She had changed out of her riding clothes and into a loose white summer dress, with white lace-up shoes with low heels.

"The maid who cleans the rooms," said Szczygiel. "She found the bed had been slept in. What is more, the towels were damp. Whoever it was took a bath, too."

"You are thinking it could have been our murderer. The gate guards didn't see him leave the White House because he didn't leave the White House."

"Exactly. And that, I think, limits him to a member of the staff. When he came down this morning, no one paid him any attention. They were accustomed to seeing him around."

"He could have had many reasons for sleeping on the third floor," said Mrs. Roosevelt.

"Without saying anything to anyone? He might have told the usher there was a guest on the third floor."

"But we have no idea who he was? Or that he *was* a he."

"Lieutenant Kennelly has men up there dusting for fingerprints."

"Well—"

"It may not amount to anything, but it's all the lead we have at the moment."

IV

1

MRS. ROOSEVELT'S STUDY WAS a capacious and comfortable room significantly larger than her bedroom. Other First Ladies usually reversed the arrangement, slept in this bigger room, and kept a sitting room in the office where Mrs. Roosevelt slept.

But Mrs. Roosevelt handled an extensive correspondence and was involved in other business, and she chose to make the larger room her study. She worked at an antique desk she had brought down from New York City. The room was decorated with family pictures and ship models. Her secretary, Malvina "Tommy" Thompson—"the woman who makes my life possible"—took dictation from a chair to one side of the desk. She was roughly the same age as Mrs. Roosevelt and was almost as close to her as Missy was to the president.

Tommy scanned the mail and made judgments as to which pieces deserved the First Lady's immediate attention and which could wait. She marked passages in documents delivered for Mrs. Roosevelt to read. She found time to skim the newspapers and to mark items she thought the First Lady ought to see. Sometimes she clipped an article and attached it to the front page of a newspaper.

A little after noon, Tommy answered the telephone, covered the mouthpiece with her hand, and said, "Mr. Szczygiel would like to see you. Lieutenant Kennelly is with him."

"Call for them," said Mrs. Roosevelt. "And order some lunch. Tell Mrs. Nesbitt to include some spirits on the tray. Our gentlemen drink, and though I don't feel easy about it, they are working long and hard, and I suppose we should accommodate them."

While she waited for the two men, she read an article about geophagists in the South. They were people who ate clay. Suffering from malnutrition, they swallowed clay, probably motivated by an instinct that it afforded them nutrients they should have been getting from vegetables but did not because their diets were confined, by choice or necessity, to fatback, the meat from squirrels and opossums, and an occasional catfish, plus corn pone and hominy grits. She put a note on the article that Tommy should forward it to Harry Hopkins—who had probably seen it.

The two men arrived.

"A bit of progress," said Szczygiel. He opened a duffel

bag and pulled out a pair of coveralls and a pair of rubber boots, exactly like the ones he and Kennelly had worn to explore the tunnel. "They were in the shrubbery—I mean, duffel bag and contents—outside the north side of the East Room. And that's not all. Out on the lawn . . . a knife. I'd guess it was pitched from the roof, as far as a man could throw it."

"Let me see the knife," said Mrs. Roosevelt.

"It's gone to the coroner, who will measure it against the wounds on the body. It's a big knife, much like the bayonets soldiers attach to their rifles."

"It could have been thrown from a window," said the First Lady.

Ed Kennelly grinned. "For fifteen minutes we watched uniformed officers throwing things from windows and the roof. It looked ridiculous, but I think the experiment proved that the knife was thrown from the roof. You see, the higher up you are, the farther you can throw something. It has to do with the arc formed when the energy applied to the object acts against gravity. None of the men could throw an object weighing as much as the knife as far out as it was, except when they threw from the roof. I'm convinced it was thrown from the roof."

"I am persuaded," said Mrs. Roosevelt. "Of course, one has easy access to the roof from the third floor."

"Exactly," said Szczygiel. "But . . . only someone with knowledge of the interior layout of the White House would know that."

"I assume, then, you gentlemen have developed a scenario."

"It's speculative," said Kennelly, "but let's go through it."

Mrs. Roosevelt nodded. Someone knocked on the door. "Ah," she said. "I've ordered lunch for us."

A serving cart, wheeled up from the kitchen by a waiter, carried a plate of tuna-salad sandwiches, carrots and radishes, and flasks of what the First Lady judged to be gin and whiskey. A small bucket of ice sat on the cart, also a silver pot of coffee.

"The president despises tuna salad," said the First Lady. "But it is nutritious and economical, so I am afraid he gets it a great deal more often than he could wish. Anyway . . . your scenario, gentlemen."

Kennelly spoke. "Our man knows the White House. He comes in through one of the drainage tunnels. He could come up onto the ground floor at a number of places, through manholes. Stan and I guess he came up somewhere in the east end of the building. He was wearing the coveralls to move in the tunnel and was carrying his regular clothes in the duffel bag. He changed somewhere—"

"Maybe in the men's bathroom," Szczygiel interrupted. "He'd know there would be nobody in there at that time of night. It's used chiefly by guests coming down from an affair in the East Room."

"So, he changes his clothes," said Mrs. Roosevelt. "And then what . . . ?"

“He stashes the duffel bag,” said Kennelly. “He’d know a lot of places where he could do that. Closets . . .”

“Then he goes upstairs,” said Szczygiel. “He avoids every security man until he comes to Officer Douglas Douglas. The officer is not alerted because he knows this man. The man approaches him, maybe smiling and offering his hand to shake. And then he pulls the knife and *kills* Officer Douglas.”

“But he did not attempt to kill the president,” said Mrs. Roosevelt.

“I think you had a reasonable explanation for that, Ma’am,” said Szczygiel. “He heard voices from inside the president’s bedroom and assumed the president was not alone.”

“And what he was hearing,” she said, “was the soundtrack of the film the president was watching. I’m afraid our scenario becomes a little bit fanciful.”

“Well . . . now,” said Kennelly. “He wants to leave, as quickly as possible. He hurries down to where he has stashed his coveralls; but he looks out the window and—my God!—he sees flashes of lightning. It’s raining! The drainage tunnels will be full of water. He can’t get out of the White House except by going past a security desk.”

“So,” said the First Lady, “you theorize that he made his way up to the third floor and took one of the vacant bedrooms.”

“After shoving the duffel bag out a window,” said Szczygiel.

“Of course he can’t sleep,” Kennelly went on. “When

the rain stops, he is aware of it. He goes out on the roof and throws the knife as far as he can."

"Pour a couple of drinks for yourselves, gentlemen," said Mrs. Roosevelt. "You may as well relax, for we have a lot of unanswered questions to address."

"Exactly," said Kennelly. He stared for a moment into the whiskey he had poured over ice, then took a sip. "Simple questions like, who was our man, and what was his motive?"

"I put five agents to work this morning," said Szczygiel. "Their first job was to find out what staff was in the White House this Saturday morning. Their second job was to take those names to the security desks and find out how each man or woman entered the White House."

"And . . . ?"

"They haven't finished. But if someone was here who didn't check in, we'll have to ask that person a few questions."

"I quite agree. And let me know what you learn."

2

THE NEW YORK YANKEES were in town to play the Washington Senators. The game would begin at two o'clock, and the president had arranged for two of the Yankees to meet with him for a few minutes in the Oval Office at one.

"I am, after all, a New Yorker bred and born, and I have always taken a special interest in the Yankees."

The two Yankees invited to meet him were Babe Ruth and Lou Gehrig. Mrs. Roosevelt came to meet them, too.

Ruth was awkward. He could not quite figure out what to do with his tweed cap, which he had been wearing with an ill-fitting cream-white double-breasted suit. He held the cap in his hands before him.

He had little education and was socially inept. Apart from his outstanding record as a ballplayer, he was known for a quote. Having been told that he was demanding more salary than President Hoover made, Ruth replied, "Well, I had a better season than he did."

Gehrig had attended Columbia University and was more poised. He was the son of Germans who had come to America in the last generation. Ruth was all but garish. Gehrig was almost shy. In 1927, when Ruth hit sixty home runs, Gehrig had a better batting average and batted in more runs. People knowledgeable about baseball agreed that he, not the flamboyant Ruth, was the Yankees' most valuable player.

There was a degree of tension between the two. Until the arrival of Gehrig in 1925, Ruth was accustomed to being the star of the Yankees. He was not entirely pleased to have a rival.

"Well, you had a great season last year," said the president.

"I guess we showed the Cubs," said Ruth. They had

won the World Series over the Chicago Cubs in 1932. " 'Course now, Mr. President, you had a pretty good season yourself."

FDR laughed heartily. "Enough to get me a salary like yours?" he asked.

"You sure did hit a home run in November," said Ruth.

"Tell me, Mr. Gehrig," said Mrs. Roosevelt. "Are things better in your old neighborhood?" She meant the streets of New York, where he had grown up.

"Not much, Ma'am," said Gehrig quietly. "I will say one thing. People have hope now, which they didn't have before."

"I'm coming out to the ball game this afternoon," said the president. "And right now we're holding you away from batting practice. So . . . I'll see you on the field. Best of luck to you."

3

AFTER THE TWO BALLPLAYERS left, the president spoke to Mrs. Roosevelt. "I believe you are intermeddling in police business, Babs. Please leave the Hawkshawing to the Hawkshaws."

"We have a certain interest in this matter, Franklin," she said. "If it is handled badly, we will look like fools. I am just keeping track of what the investigators are doing, not interfering."

"Well . . . limit yourself to that, please."

The First Lady returned to her study. She had told Tommy to go home for the rest of the weekend. But she found someone waiting for her. It was Lorena Hickock.

Hick strode across the room and embraced Mrs. Roosevelt. She kissed her. "Oh, Pussy, I have missed you so," she whispered.

"I've missed you, too, my dearest Hick. You know how much I love you and how difficult life is when you are in New York."

"I save your dear letters," said Hick. "I read them over and over."

"And I yours."

Although the two women embraced and kissed and declared their love for one another, there was no carnal relationship between them. Mrs. Roosevelt was a nineteenth-century woman, educated in an English girls' school, and women of her century and background did embrace and kiss each other and did declare their love. It was platonic love. Alice Roosevelt Longworth embraced and kissed her women friends.

On the other hand, the First Lady was lonely in Washington. Lorena Hickock was the friend in whom she could confide. She confided to Hick shortly after the election of 1932 that she did not want to be First Lady and that, if she were selfish, she might regret that Franklin had been elected.

Hick was a journalist. They had met during the campaign. Mrs. Roosevelt wanted Hick to take a federal job and move into one of the rooms on the third floor of the White House. Hick did not want to give up her career.

Lorena Hickock was a woman referred to as horsy—by those who meant to be kind to her. She was bulky. Very few saw anything attractive about her.

"Oh, Hick, something *awful* has happened! Last night there was—apparently—an attempt to assassinate Franklin. Someone killed a White House police officer just outside Franklin's bedroom door. Why he didn't crash into the bedroom and kill the president is unclear. It may have something to do with the fact that Missy was showing the president a film, and the would-be assassin was frightened away by the voices on the soundtrack, which he may have taken to be real."

"You are keeping this a secret," said Hick.

"Not from you, my darling. I have complete confidence that you won't publish it."

"Sit down, Pussy. Let me massage your neck and shoulders. You are full of tension."

4

IN MID-AFTERNOON STAN SZCZYGIEL called on the telephone. He said he and Ed Kennelly would like to talk with the First Lady. Hick said she would go to a hotel, but Mrs. Roosevelt insisted she stay in the White House and called the usher to install her in a comfortable room on the third floor.

"On a condition," said Hick. "That we go out to dinner so I don't have to eat any of Mrs. Nesbitt's ghastly cooking. I don't see how Frank can endure that woman's slop day after day."

"He doesn't care anything about food," said Mrs. Roosevelt.

"Yes, you once said you could serve him scrambled eggs every night for a week and he wouldn't notice."

"Scrambled eggs are all I know how to cook," Mrs. Roosevelt protested with a shy smile.

"I think you underestimate your husband's taste for good meals," said Hick.

"Well . . . Once when we were in Albany I almost threw in the garbage some pheasants that had been sent as a gift to Franklin. I didn't know they were supposed to 'ripen' and took them for simply spoiled."

Hick went up to her third-floor room, and Szczygiel and Kennelly arrived shortly.

"We have something," said Szczygiel. "You remember I said we would find out which staff members were in the White House this morning and then check that against the security desks, to find out when everyone entered. Well . . . There was one in the West Wing this morning who checked out at the West Wing security desk last evening at eight-forty-six and checked in again this morning. But he did not leave the grounds through any of the gates last evening or enter through a gate this morning. This suggests he was in the White House all night."

"And who might that be?"

"A lawyer named Ben Hay. He works for Mr. Ickes at the Department of the Interior, but for now he's on temporary assignment to the president. He works at drafting bills."

"Appointed—But that means he could not have come here before March. We've defined our culprit as someone who knows the White House intimately."

"He was on the White House staff of President Coolidge, then on the White House staff of President Hoover. He could very well know every nook and cranny of this place, including security routines and all the rest of it. He could very well have known Officer Douglas Douglas."

"What's more, he's a Republican," said Kennelly.

"Appointed by Mr. Ickes. Well . . . Mr. Ickes is a moderate Republican, from New York. Mr. Hay . . . ?"

"Is from New York," said Szczygiel. "He's forty-three years old, a graduate of Columbia University. He graduated from law school in nineteen-thirteen and went into practice with Root, Ballantine. He enlisted in the army in nineteen-seventeen and was commissioned a second lieutenant. When he was discharged in nineteen-nineteen, he went back to his firm. In nineteen-twenty-six he was appointed as counsel to President Calvin Coolidge. President Hoover kept him on. President Roosevelt did not, but Mr. Ickes called him back to Washington. Mr. Ickes, it appears, has a great deal of respect for him."

"Is there any record of association with . . . radicals?" asked the First Lady.

"We're looking," said Szczygiel.

"He fits every element of the scenario," said Kennelly. "He knows the White House. The White House knows him."

"You could not arrest him on this evidence," said the First Lady solemnly.

"No," said Kennelly. "But at least we have a suspect. We'll keep him under surveillance and continue the background check."

5

HICK HAD A VERY firm idea about where she wanted to go for dinner. They took an inconspicuous White House car, with driver. Stan Szczygiel accompanied them as Secret Service escort. They crossed the Potomac and soon were in rural Virginia. Mrs. Roosevelt quickly lost her bearings, but Hick knew the roads and gave directions to the driver.

The First Lady was supposed to be incognito. She wore an ample white turban wrapped around her head and a pair of dark glasses with horn rims, and she clenched in her mouth a short amber cigarette holder with an unlit cigarette.

She learned their destination only when they reached

it. When she saw what it was, she did not want to go in. Hick laughed and urged her on.

It was an illegal club, of the kind called carpet joints because they had carpets on the floors as most roadhouses did not. There would be gambling inside, and liquor, and God knew what else.

"If I am seen here—"

"You'll be seen in good company," said Hick.

The joint was called the Clock because it was identified to the knowledgeable by a big clock lighted by red bulbs. Not just anyone could get in. But when Hick identified herself, the door was opened, and shortly the manager came to the foyer.

"Hick!" he said. "Nice to see you! And here are—Let me guess. Mr. and Mrs. Trumble!"

"Got dinner for us, Ollie?"

"You better believe it. And a table that's discrete, yet has a good view of the stage."

Their table was against the wall on the right side of the dining room and under an overhang that cast a deep shadow over it. Ollie blew out the candle burning in a small lamp.

"Steaks," he said. "With a first-class Bordeaux. And first-class drinks before."

When he had left the table, Mrs. Roosevelt shook her head. "We violate the Prohibition law in the privacy of the White House, as we did in Albany. Franklin wouldn't have it any other way. But here, I—I am not sure."

"Hey, relax," said Hick. "Relax, Puss. You deserve a night off duty."

"That is true," said Szczygiel dryly.

Bright lights came up on the stage, and a tall young woman with bleached, marcelled hair appeared, to raucous applause. She began to dance to the jazz music of a quintet of Negro musicians. After a moment she began to unzip her tight red dress.

"My Lord! Is she going to—?"

"Strip," said Hick. "Yes, she's going to strip."

A waiter appeared and put down three generous drinks. "Glenlivet . . ." he whispered.

"Tell Ollie thanks," said Hick.

Mrs. Roosevelt stared into her glass, where an amber liquid covered two small ice cubes. "I'm not certain I can drink this," she said. "Apart from the law, I've no experience with it. I shouldn't want to get sick."

"You better, Puss," said Hick. "It's a single-malt Scotch and damned expensive. You'll offend the hell out of Ollie if you don't drink it. And me, too."

The First Lady sniffed at the liquid, then took a small, tentative sip of it.

"That's it," said Szczygiel. "Sippin' whiskey. You'd never belt *that* down."

By now the dancer on the stage had removed her dress and tossed it aside, revealing her pale, smooth body, now covered only by a brassiere and a pair of skimpy panties from which a narrow drape of pink chiffon hung to her ankles. Her navel was exposed, and she was gyrating her hips and sometimes imperiously thrusting them forward.

"That's called bump and grind," Hick explained.

"I can see the origin of the allusion," said Mrs. Roosevelt dryly.

"Look around," said Szczygiel. "I think you'll see some people you recognize. Don't worry about them recognizing you. They're absorbed in what they're doing."

"That pair are," said Hick, nodding toward two men sitting at a table in the shadow of the overhang and two tables forward from the one where the First Lady sat.

The two men all but ignored the performance on the stage. They were absorbed in each other. Faces close, they whispered and seemed to amuse each other immensely.

"J. Edgar Hoover and Clyde Tolson," said Szczygiel.

The girl on the stage removed her brassiere and showed her small, firm breasts, to the applause of most of the audience.

"How far does she . . . ?" asked Mrs. Roosevelt.

"All the way," said Hick. "All the way."

It was true. After a few minutes of dancing with her breasts exposed, the young woman slipped down the only covering that remained to her and strutted around the stage stark naked.

"I've heard of this sort of thing," said Mrs. Roosevelt. "I had supposed they left *something* to the imagination."

"Usually they do," said Hick. "They don't go this far

at the Gayety, over in the city. But this place is illegal every other way, so—"

"There's gambling upstairs," said Szczygiel. "Brothers Hoover and Tolson will be going up there soon."

The naked girl scampered off the stage. A voice boomed over a loudspeaker—

"LADIES AND GENTLEMEN! SISTER AIMEE!"

A statuesque blond woman, substantially older than the girl who had just left the stage, came out.

"I cannot, I *do not* believe this," said Mrs. Roosevelt.

"Believe it," said Hick. "She's Aimee Semple McPherson, the big California evangelist."

"But why?"

"She fell on hard times for a while," said Hick. "You remember she disappeared for a while in nineteen-twenty-six. The story was, she had been kidnapped. When the truth came out, it was that she was shacked up with a boyfriend. That disillusioned a lot of the suckers in her temple congregation. After that she had marital problems. She's defendant in a half million dollars' worth of lawsuits—"

"But doing this won't make her enough money to—"

"No," said Hick. "It certainly will not. She appears in private clubs all around the country, six or eight weeks a year. She's never advertised. The word gets around. She's why I wanted us to come here tonight."

Aimee Semple McPherson began a dance much like the one her predecessor had done and shortly unzipped her dress and began to tease that she was going to remove it. The crowd cheered and urged her on—"Take it off! Take it off!"

"I still don't understand her motive," said Mrs. Roosevelt. "Why would she—?"

"It's really quite simple," said Hick. "Dear Sister Aimee is an *exhibitionist.*"

"And an ecdysiast," said Szczygiel sarcastically.

"Look at her," said Hick. "She's ecstatic!"

By the time their steaks and wine were on the table, Aimee Semple McPherson was strutting around nude. But Hoover and Tolson hardly noticed.

V

1

IT WAS A BURDEN for the president to leave the White House and go to church on Sunday mornings. Mrs. Roosevelt had no great interest in going if he was not. Later in the morning she would go to the funeral home and convey her personal condolences to Mrs. Douglas. But for now, she sat in bed much later than was her wont, sipping coffee from her breakfast tray and going through the Sunday-morning papers. Hick sat nearby, eating from a tray and reading newspapers.

The president was doing the same. Missy was with him. When she saw something she thought interesting, she would hand him the section of the newspaper with that item and suggest he read it.

They took their news from the papers, not from radio. Besides the *Washington Post*, several other East Coast newspapers were delivered early at the White House, having come by train. The president liked to scan the

Boston Globe, the *New York Times*, the New York *Sun*, the *Philadelphia Inquirer*, and the Baltimore *Sun*. Later trains would bring papers from farther west, such as the Cleveland *Plain Dealer* and the *Cincinnati Enquirer*. Still later trains would bring the *Chicago Daily News*.

President Roosevelt believed that 80 percent of American newspapers had opposed his election and opposed him yet. He would not so much as look at the vitriolic *Chicago Tribune*, published and controlled by the megalomaniacal Bertie McCormick. Actually, the president was not opposed by all that many newspapers, only by a slender majority. Many newspapers held him in awe. Even opposing papers found him fascinating, as they did his First Lady.

The *New York Times* editorialized that FDR had turned the national emergency into a personal triumph. "He seemed to be riding the whirlwind and directing the storm."

"I see Sam Leibowitz is up to his armpits in the Scottsboro case," said Missy. "Too bad you can't send him best wishes."

"Price of being president," said FDR.

The Scottsboro Nine were young Negro men accused of raping two white girls who were riding with them in a boxcar. In spite of the fact that a doctor had examined the girls and testified they had not been raped, the jury convicted all nine, including one who was only twelve years old, and all were sentenced to death. The Supreme Court of the United States had reversed the convictions on the ground that the young men had not had effective counsel—their attorney not having called a single witness on their behalf. Famed New York lawyer Samuel Leibowitz had been persuaded to take over the case and seek a new trial.

"Negro men accused of raping white girls," said Missy. "They can't be rational about that, down South."

"Sam will take care of it," said the president calmly. "Look here. They're going to use light from a distant star to switch on the earthly lights at the Chicago World's Fair. That light's been on its way here for billions of years. I wonder what it would think, if light could think, that after all these years and all those miles, it is being captured in a telescope and juiced up by electrical devices so it can trip a switch in Chicago."

"It almost seems like sacrilege to interrupt it," said Missy.

"Well, I suppose that star has plenty and more to spare."

2

ED KENNELLY HAD ASKED the New York Police Department for a report on Ben Hay. A wire arrived Sunday before noon.

> This department has no record on Mr. Ben Hay. He has never been arrested in this city, nor

has he been the subject of any criminal complaint.

In 1931 he was a witness for the prosecution in the criminal trial of one Arthur Flegenheimer (Dutch Schultz), who was charged with murder. Mr. Hay's testimony was limited to the question of whether or not Mr. Flegenheimer was present at a party where he said he had been present at the time of the shooting, which was Mr. Flegenheimer's alibi. Mr. Hay testified that Mr. Flegenheimer was not present, though three other witnesses testified that he was, so he was acquitted. The party was at Polly Adler's. Other guests at this party, incidentally, were Charles "Lucky" Luciano, Frank Costello, and Meyer Lansky.

Stan Szczygiel frowned over the wire, brought to him by Kennelly. "Polly Adler's . . . Polly Adler . . . Some way the name strikes a chord, but I'm not sure who Polly Adler is."

Kennelly grinned. "She's the madam of this country's most notorious house of ill reputey."

"Oh, yes. I remember."

"Everybody who is anybody in New York visits Polly's sooner or later."

Szczygiel tipped his head to one side. "Well . . . Not everybody, I should think."

"If you think you're café society, you go to the Stork

Club, where you can associate with the likes of the ex-con Sherman Billingsley and the other felons who hang out there. If you're more democratic, you party at Polly's."

"So what does this tell us about Ben Hay?"

"That he's nobody's innocent," said Kennelly. "The guys who were at that same party were the top guys of the New York Mob."

"Maybe he just likes what Polly has to offer."

"I'm going to look into that," said Kennelly.

3

A LITTLE AFTER TWO that afternoon, Kennelly arrived at a house on M Street, an address he knew well.

Washington had its own Polly Adler. Her name was Roberta Asman, but she was called Bobby. Her big white frame house on M Street was unprepossessing. The paint was peeling. The dilapidated eaves gutters let sheets of water cascade during a rain. The littered front yard was covered with weeds, not grass. This was how Bobby wanted it. The house looked like others in the neighborhood and attracted no attention.

Bobby did attract attention by generous gifts to neighborhood charities. She supported the soup kitchen in the basement of the First Methodist Church, providing 90 percent of all the money it got. She gave money to send city children out for a week in the country. Bobby's bus, so-called, cruised the neighborhood and picked up elderly people to take them to the stores.

Kennelly rang the bell. A maid appeared. He showed her his badge and told her he wanted to talk to Miss Asman.

Bobby appeared. She was a tall, slender woman with coal-black hair, black eyebrows, and dark brown eyes. She wore false eyelashes and a heavy covering of bright-red lipstick. Her clinging black silk nightgown was held up by spaghetti straps.

"Hi, Ed. What brings *you* out here?"

"No problem for you, Bobby," he said. "Just like to ask a few questions."

"Sure. C'min."

She led him past the reception parlor and to a small sitting room behind it.

If her house was unprepossessing outside, it was lush inside. It was adorned in what many people called Whorehouse Gothic, meaning that it was embellished in dark reds—drapes, wallpaper, rugs, upholstery—and gilt. Since the drapes were all closed, the rooms were lighted by bulbs in milk-glass globes and by bridge lamps.

"I'm surprised you're all this busy on Sunday afternoon," said Kennelly.

Bobby used tongs to put ice cubes in two glasses, then poured gin over that ice. "Sunday! That's when your office worker has a day off. And that's when my ladies have their biggest days."

He had seen three of her "ladies" in the reception

parlor. She hired no shopworn, garish girls. Shown off in a sort of uniform—white semi-sheer teddies—they were appealing; and if he hadn't been a happily married man, and religious to boot, he might have been tempted.

"Any senators in the house this afternoon?" he asked playfully.

She grinned. "Now, Ed . . ." She was known for her discretion, on which many prominent men relied.

"I do have to ask you about a man," he said.

"Aww, Ed."

"Police business, strictly."

"You understand I don't know who all the men are who come here. I guess I don't know who half of them are. Less than that. I don't know who a quarter of them are. In and out. You know."

"If this guy comes in, he comes in often. I got his name from Polly Adler." That was not exactly true, of course; but Mark Twain had put in the mouth of Huckleberry Finn the philosophy that circumstances allowed a man to tell a few "stretchers." Ed sipped gin. "The man has been in Washington a few years and works for the government. But he's well connected in New York. I mean, *well* connected."

"Like with who?"

Another stretcher: "Like with, say, Lucky Luciano and Frank Costello."

Bobby whistled. "So . . . police business. Homicide business. Got nothing to do with me."

"Nothing to do with you. I just want to know if the guy comes in here or not."

"Who is he?"

"Ben Hay."

"Ben—Yeah, Ben comes in here. He's a bachelor. He—"

"What about that party he held here?" Ed ventured. It was a guess, a flyer, but—

Bobby shook her head. "You know everything." She smiled. "We're a pair of pros, you and me. I guess you're as good in your line as I am in mine."

"I'm complimented, Bobby."

"So intended," she said.

"So who came to the party?"

"You probably know anyway. Dutch Schultz—"

"Dutch Schultz came to a party held by Ben Hay?" Ed asked, thinking of Hay's testimony against Schultz in his 1931 murder trial. "What year was that?"

"Uh . . . couple of—no, *three* years ago. It was nineteen-thirty. Anyway, Meyer Lansky was here. He spends some time in Washington, though he hardly ever comes to Bobby's place. He's got a carpet joint over in Virginia, called the Clock. And there were guys I didn't know."

"How many, all told?"

"Oh . . . eight . . . ten."

"Who paid?"

"Ben did. He paid for a lady to entertain each guy, plus drinks, plus eats."

"Why? Did you ever figure out?"

"Well, they sent the ladies out of the room for a while, so they could have a private confab. That took no more than twenty minutes. Lansky didn't go upstairs with his lady that night. He was newly married."

"Party cost a piece of money, didn't it?" Ed asked.

"*I'd* call it a piece of money."

"And Hay paid."

"In cash."

4

STAN SZCZYGIEL SAT AT his desk, interviewing a uniformed officer. "Let's go over this again," he said.

"Yes, Sir. You asked us to check our logs and identify anyone who was present in the Executive Wing on Saturday morning who had not checked in. We gave you the name of Mr. Hay."

"Correct."

"Well . . . It occurred to me and Officer Lucas that there was another something that might be irregular. Suppose somebody checked in on Saturday morning who hadn't checked out Friday evening. Would that be something you'd want to know about?"

"Definitely."

"Okay. Miss Angela Patchen checked in the reg'lar way Saturday morning, through the northwest gate. She came through the North Portico and checked at the desk when she went out to the Executive Wing. But how she got out the night before, we have no record. So far as the log shows, she was in the Executive Wing all night. But she wasn't, because she came in off Pennsylvania Avenue on Saturday morning."

"She's a secretary, I believe," said Szczygiel.

"Yes, Sir. She works for Mr. Hopkins and Mr. Tug-well."

"Okay, thanks. I'll look into it."

The Executive Wing was not deserted on Sunday af-ternoon. The New Dealers had brought with them a new set of work habits. Szczygiel went to the personnel files and pulled the jacket on Angela Patchen.

Patchen, Angela Silvana

1320 H Street, N.W.

B. Columbus, Ohio, 13 January 1903, daughter of Giuseppe Paccinelli (changed to Joseph Patchen, 1900) and Silvana Brunicardi.

Graduated Central High School, 1921. Employed, secretary, City of Columbus, 1921-1925. Employed secretary to Sherman Elliott, Office of the President, 1925-1929. Secretary to Milton Forbes, 1929-1933. Employed secretary to Rexford Tug-well and Harry Hopkins, 1933-.

Recommended to Sherman Elliott by Congressman John Vorys and Mayor Joseph Dugan.

Unmarried.

Efficiency: excellent to good.

Negative reports: none.

The file also contained the letter by which Representative John Vorys introduced Angela Patchen to Sherman Elliott—

This will introduce you to Miss Angela Patchen, a lifelong resident of Columbus whose family is well known to me.

Mr. Joseph Patchen was, prior to Prohibition, a brewer and produced an extraordinarily fine light lager. When the brewing of beer became illegal, he turned the fleet of trucks that had formerly delivered kegs of beer to general hauling and soon acquired a deserved reputation for honesty and efficiency.

He has been, needless to say, a staunch Republican and was active in bringing out the vote of the Italian-American community for the election of President Coolidge. In addition, he makes a generous monthly contribution to the GOP committee.

```
    If you can employ Miss Patchen or
help her to find suitable employment in
Washington, it will be well received in
this community.
```

5

"SHE DIDN'T SIGN OUT Friday evening, yet she signed in on Saturday morning," Szczygiel said to Mrs. Roosevelt and Ed Kennelly.

He had asked if she would have time to see him that Sunday afternoon. She made time. He called Ed and asked him to join him for the meeting with the First Lady.

"An oversight?" asked Mrs. Roosevelt. "Some officer forgot to—"

"I'm not going to say our people are infallible," said Szczygiel. "God knows they aren't." He shrugged. "Who is? But I don't think we miss many of these."

"She could hardly be a suspect in the death of Officer Douglas Douglas," said the First Lady. "I mean, a girl could hardly have plunged a knife repeatedly into—"

"Let's don't write that off as impossible, Ma'am," said Kennelly. "The female of the species—I've seen big, strong men stabbed or bludgeoned to death by little slips of girls. It's a matter of her catching him off guard."

"A possibility . . ." Szczygiel mused. "She could have distracted Douglas while a man stepped up and stabbed him."

"That would be easier to imagine if he had been stabbed in the back," said Mrs. Roosevelt.

"We're getting a little ahead of things, to call this girl a suspect," said Kennelly.

"We haven't got much more against Ben Hay," said the First Lady.

"Well . . ." said Kennelly. "It turns out that Hay has some odd friends, and he also seems to have a good deal more money than he's making as a White House lawyer."

"A secret life?" asked Mrs. Roosevelt.

"Not exactly secret. In nineteen-thirty-one he testified for the prosecution in the murder trial of Dutch Schultz. Still, a year before that he held a fancy party at Bobby Asman's—Do you know who Bobby Asman is, Ma'am?"

"I'm afraid I don't."

"Bobby Asman is a big, successful madam here in Washington. The city's leading madam. She's almost as famous as Polly Adler. Anyway, Ben Hay had a dinner and so on at Bobby's, and one of his guests was Dutch Schultz. Expensive party. Dutch should have been honored. Maybe was. But a year later Ben Hay is testifying against the Dutchman in a trial in New York."

"All of which has to do with what, Lieutenant Kennelly?"

"Another guest at the party was Meyer Lansky. Do you know who Meyer Lansky is?"

"I . . . Yes. I've heard the name."

"Lansky is the brains behind a lot of Mob operations. He doesn't seem to be into bootlegging much, but he is big in gambling. He runs carpet joints. He has one over in Virginia, called the Clock. They say he knows how to run a joint. He's run them in Fort Lauderdale, Sarasota, and so on. Illegal gambling. Illegal liquor. Prostitution in rooms upstairs. Usually some kind of a show. Some big names have appeared on Lansky's stages. Louis Armstrong. Bing Crosby. Rudy Vallee. He pays well."

"And I return to my question," she said. "What has any of this to do with the death of Officer Douglas Douglas? And, more specifically, what does it have to do with the murder's having occurred just outside the president's bedroom?"

"That will be very difficult to establish," said Ed Kennelly. "I can speculate."

"Please do."

"By the end of the year, Prohibition will be no more. That means there will be no more bootleggers. That means that a billion-dollar industry will disappear in a puff of smoke. There are people who hold that against the president." Kennelly shrugged. "Prohibition would have been repealed even if Hoover had been reelected. But many don't see it that way. Many feel that the president led the fight for repeal and is responsible for the demise of their illicit businesses."

"Alright," said Stan Szczygiel. "You can establish a connection between Ben Hay and the Mob. I'd call him an unlikely hit man, though."

"He had one essential advantage," said Kennelly.

"Being?" asked Mrs. Roosevelt.

"Access," said Kennelly.

6

HICK ALL BUT REFUSED to eat the fare sent up from the White House kitchen. If she could not lure the First Lady out for a Sunday-night dinner, she would have something delivered from a restaurant. That evening she joined the president and Missy and Harry Hopkins for the cocktail hour. Mrs. Roosevelt was there too, of course.

"Mr. President," said Hick—more often she called him Frank—"is there nothing you can do about Mrs. Nesbitt?"

"Babs loves her," said the president.

Mrs. Henrietta Nesbitt was a Hudson Valley neighbor recruited by the First Lady to be deputy chatelaine of the Roosevelt White House. She was a stern, humorless woman who wore her hair bound up in a bun, and she was the most unimaginative cook imaginable. White House meals were a Washington joke. Everyone dreaded and everyone avoided if possible a small dinner, or a luncheon, at the presidential mansion.

"Mrs. Nesbitt performs her functions very capably," said Mrs. Roosevelt. "The chief desideratum in this establishment is saving money. We do not keep within the food budget as it is. We are spending our own money. Without Mrs. Nesbitt, I shudder to think how much the kitchen would spend."

"I've considered issuing an executive order to the White House police, not to admit her to the grounds," said the president dryly.

"Since when did you become a gourmand, Franklin?" asked Mrs. Roosevelt.

"I have always appreciated good food," he said. "And God knows I see little enough of it."

"I told you he liked things besides scrambled eggs," Hick said to the First Lady.

"Pish and tish," said Mrs. Roosevelt.

"Well . . . Eleanor and I are going out to dinner," said Hick firmly. "I will order something brought you from the restaurant kitchen. All you need do is alert the gate guards that it is coming."

The president and Missy did not watch a movie that night. When the First Lady and Lorena Hickock had left, Missy went up to her suite on the third floor and changed into a dark-blue silk nightgown covered with a white organdy peignoir.

While they waited for the promised delivery of restaurant food, they listened to a radio broadcast of the opera *Fidelio*. Later they would listen to records.

The food came as promised: beef stroganoff, a salad, a bottle of Bordeaux, a Key lime pie.

"I guess we can trust the kitchen to make the coffee," said the president. "Mrs. Nesbitt does know how to boil water."

"And scramble eggs," said Missy.

VI

1

MRS. ROOSEVELT WAS INVARIABLY sympathetic toward young women who might be in trouble. When Stan Szczygiel said he meant to interrogate Angela Patchen, the First Lady suggested he do it in her study, over coffee and pastries.

"It will be less . . . confrontational and might generate more cooperation."

Angela Patchen was not confrontational when she faced the Secret Service agent and the First Lady, but she was not intimidated either. She was thirty years old and had worked since she was eighteen. She had the mien of a woman who had seen a good deal and coped with a good deal.

She was of medium height and somewhat more than medium weight—plump but certainly not fat. Her hair was coal-black and not marcelled, instead hanging smooth and lustrous and unstylishly long, below her ears.

Black brows arched above her dark eyes. She wore a little red lipstick and appeared to be otherwise free of cosmetics. Her black pleated skirt hung two inches or so below her knees. Her white cotton blouse was meant to fit loosely, but her breasts filled it and stretched it taut.

She thanked Mrs. Roosevelt for the coffee and stirred sugar and cream into it.

"Miss Patchen," said the First Lady, "we have a little problem and thought you might be able to help us out."

"Anything I can do," said Angela. She was not intimidated and sat comfortably balancing her cup and saucer on her knees, her legs crossed at the ankles, as if she had been taught in a girl's finishing school.

"According to the logs," said Stan Szczygiel, "you entered the White House at eight-fifteen on Saturday morning."

The young woman nodded. "We work Saturday mornings, of course. Sometimes Saturday afternoons, too."

"Yes. You entered the grounds through the northwest gate, then stopped at the security desk at the entrance to the West Wing."

"Right."

"And when you leave for the day, you go past the security desk, where your leaving is noted on the log, then you go out through the northwest gate, where the gate guard checks you out."

"That's right."

"Well, on Friday evening there is no entry in the log on the security desk to indicate that you left the West

Wing. What is more, there is no indication at the northwest gate that you left the grounds."

"I didn't go out by the northwest gate that evening. I'd called a cab, and he picked me up in the parking lot. We went through the gate onto West Executive Avenue."

"How about the West Wing security desk?"

"I don't know what the problem might be," she said. "I walked by and said good evening to the man on duty. If he didn't note it in his log, that's not my fault."

"Do you know the name of the officer?"

"Uh . . . No, I really don't. I've been here long enough that I recognize many of the White House officers, but I didn't recognize that man."

2

SZCZYGIEL CHECKED THE DUTY roster. The uniformed man at that desk that evening was Officer Frank Slye. Szczygiel confronted him.

"No, Sir," said Slye emphatically. "She did not walk past me. I would have noticed her and entered her departure in the log."

Szczygiel showed a slight smile. "She's not the kind of girl you'd overlook, is she?"

Slye smiled and shook his head. "No, Sir. I don't think I'd ever overlook Miss Patchen. Not with that chest. I mean, it's like a pair of headlights comin' toward you."

Szczygiel studied Slye critically. He had already

checked the man's personnel file. Frank Slye had worked as a uniformed White House policeman since 1920. Nothing negative appeared on his record. He was a thin man with knife-sharp features, a small scar on his cheek, brown hair, and blue eyes.

"So, you're saying she did not come past you."

"Sir, she did *not* come past my duty desk on Friday evening."

"What was your shift?"

"Four to twelve, Sir. Actually, it was not my regular shift. I was called in at the last moment to substitute for Officer McKay, who had an emergency appendectomy that afternoon."

"And Miss Patchen did not come past your security desk during those hours?"

"No, Sir, she definitely did not. I know her. Pleasant girl . . . apart from you know what. Always has a cheery word or two."

3

"COLONEL DODGE," SAID ED Kennelly into the telephone. "This is Lieutenant Edward Kennelly, D.C. police, Homicide Division."

"Ah, so. Homicide . . . What can I do for you, Lieutenant?"

"Regard this conversation as absolutely confidential, to begin with."

"Okay. I have some little experience with doing that," said the colonel dryly.

"This is just a routine inquiry."

"I doubt that any inquiry from a homicide detective is ever entirely routine."

"Well . . . I'm at a stage in an investigation where I'm just putting together all the information I can get. I am not at the accusatory stage yet."

"So who do you want to talk about?"

"Ben Hay, who served under you as a lieutenant during the war. You gave him a letter of recommendation when he moved from a firm in New York to a job in the executive offices of President Coolidge."

"Yes. Yes. I remember Hay. Is he in trouble?"

"Not necessarily. Probably not, in fact. What can you tell me about him?"

"He came to the army from a prominent New York law firm, to which I believe he returned after the war. Someone had asked for a commission for him, and he got it and was a second lieutenant when I met him. He came to me at his own request. You'd expect a young man with his background would want a post with the judge advocate general or something like that. He didn't. He wanted to serve in a combat unit, an infantry company. I was skeptical, and I really didn't have room for another lieutenant. But he made one hell of an impression. The first thing that impressed me was his physical condition. A lot of the boys coming in then were flabby. Hay had the body of an Olympic athlete."

"I hear he still does."

"I bet he does. Then he surprised me. He asked to be allowed to take special courses in hand-to-hand combat. He learned jiujitsu, for one thing. He learned dirty tricks. And he learned to kill with a knife. He used a bayonet, which he sharpened until men said you could shave with it. He slithered across no-man's-land one night and cut the throat of a German captain. It amused him to think about how horrified the Germans would be in the morning when they found their captain dead that way in their own trench."

"Good soldier, generally?"

"We gave him a Silver Star. The French awarded him their Croix de Guerre."

4

MEETING WITH STAN SZCZYGIEL and Ed Kennelly, Mrs. Roosevelt had a question. "We can't think of a motive that would inspire Miss Patchen to lie. On the other hand, Officer Slye had a motive."

"What motive do you have in mind?" asked Szczygiel.

"Well . . . We know that Miss Patchen was not in the West Wing all night. At some time or another she left, at which time she had to walk past the security desk manned by Officer Slye. When she did, he was derelict in his duty. He was supposed to enter her departure in the log, and he did not."

"Maybe she distracted him," said Szczygiel. "He admired her . . . figure."

"So much so that he would entirely forget to record her departure?"

"Maybe there was hanky-panky," Kennelly suggested.

"Still . . ." said the First Lady. "She didn't remain with him at his desk until he went off duty at midnight."

"Or did she?" asked Kennelly.

"She didn't," said Szczygiel. "I checked with the man who was on duty at the west gate. She was picked up by a taxi, just as she said."

"At what time?" asked Mrs. Roosevelt.

"The gate log says seven-twenty-three. About the time she said."

"So there you have it," said the First Lady. "Miss Patchen left the White House at seven-twenty-three. For whatever reason—distracted by her figure, perhaps—Officer Slye omitted to do his duty to record her leaving the West Wing."

"We are talking about motive," said Szczygiel. "What would motivate Slye to falsify the log?"

"Promise of future favors," said Kennelly dismissively, betraying a little impatience with the conversation.

"That doesn't work, Lieutenant," said Mrs. Roosevelt. "Why would Miss Patchen want the log to indicate she stayed in the West Wing, when the gate log would show she left in a taxi at seven-twenty-three?"

"It's a sideshow," said Kennelly. "The girl didn't kill Officer Douglas, or help someone else do it."

"We can put the matter aside for now," said the First Lady. "I gather you have something more important to talk about."

"I had a talk with one of Ben Hay's old army buddies, from nineteen-seventeen," said Kennelly.

"How did you find him?" asked Mrs. Roosevelt.

"From Hay's personnel file. When he was originally appointed to the White House staff, under President Coolidge, he submitted letters of recommendation. One was from an army captain under whom he had served. Now a colonel—Colonel Dodge."

"And?" asked Szczygiel.

"Hay took special training in the tactics of hand-to-hand combat. He learned jiujitsu, for one thing. Also, how to use a knife. He was regarded as absolutely deadly with a bayonet. I don't mean a bayonet attached to a rifle; I mean a bayonet in hand. He didn't have thrusting in mind. He had slashing. He sharpened his bayonet razor-sharp, and one night he cut a German officer's throat."

"The bayonet found on the lawn . . ." said the First Lady. "Was it razor-sharp?"

"No. An ordinary bayonet."

"Are army bayonets common? I mean, do civilians have them?"

"Boys brought them home as souvenirs," said Szczygiel. "They couldn't bring their rifles or pistols, but usually they could get a bayonet through."

"Some odd things came home as souvenirs," said Kennelly. "When I came home, I went back to my old pool hall. A guy named Kelly had sent from France a square box. He sent it to the poolroom, with instructions it was not to be opened; he would open it himself when he got back. Well . . . Kelly didn't come back. So we opened the box. In it was a German helmet—with a skull in it."

"I'm sorry you told that story," said Mrs. Roosevelt.

"I'm sorry," said Kennelly. "The point is, Hay was an athlete, trained to use a knife to kill, and he was no fading flower; he had a lot of courage."

"And does that make him the man who killed Officer Douglas?"

"No. But it means he was capable of it."

"Perhaps it's time to ask Mr. Hay a few questions."

5

"MR. HAY," SAID ED Kennelly. "You're a lawyer, so I'm sure you know your rights."

Once more, the confrontation between the investigators and a suspect took place in Mrs. Roosevelt's study. It was less likely to be noticed, she said.

Ben Hay did not look like a man who had killed a White House officer with a knife. He was something like five-feet-nine and growing bald. Obviously he carefully combed the strands of his hair across his head, but it was a losing struggle to conceal the fact that there was not much hair left. His chiseled, innocent-looking face was long and strong, with a cleft chin. Except for the vanishing of his hair, he looked vaguely like the unrealistically handsome men who appeared in Arrow Shirt ads.

"You are a well-informed man," said Ed Kennelly. "I assume you know what happened in the White House Friday night."

"I understand there is great interest in keeping it confidential," said Hay. "And you can be assured I have mentioned it to no one."

"We are confident you understand the circumstances," said the First Lady.

"So, Mr. Hay," said Kennelly. "A check of the logs shows that you left the Executive Wing about half past eight. You did not, however, leave the White House grounds. The gate guards made no note of you. This morning you checked into the Executive Wing without having entered the grounds through the gates. Do you have an explanation for that?"

Hay settled a scornful gaze on the Irish cop. Plainly he did not hold the type in high regard and judged he was a blunderer. "Easy enough," he said. "When I left the West Wing I found it was raining—raining cats and dogs, as they say. I had no great interest in getting soaked. So, I walked into the first floor. I stopped in the kitchen and picked up a tuna-salad sandwich and a tumbler of gin—which, incidentally, it was difficult to pry loose. Then I took the West Elevator to the third floor. I knew that at least one of the guest suites would be vacant. I knocked on a door. Finding the rooms vacant, I went in and made myself comfortable for the night."

"And this morning?" asked Kennelly.

"I reversed my course," said Hay calmly. "I used the West Elevator—Elevator Number One, it's called—and went down to the first floor. On my way across to the Executive Wing I caught up with the president, who was wheeling himself to his office. I caught up with him, and we exchanged pleasantries. Simple."

"Is it your custom to sleep in the guest rooms?" asked Szczygiel.

"Custom? No, but it's not the first time I've done it. I've done it three other times since March fourth. Sometimes we work late. Very late. The president's legislative program requires a lot of careful drafting. We can be sure that whatever we do, it will be challenged on the Hill."

"Did you know Officer Douglas Douglas?" Szczygiel asked.

Hay smiled. "I know you, Stan. We've been around here a long time—you much longer than I. Yes, I knew Doug Douglas. We used to make jokes about his name."

"He was stabbed with a bayonet," said Szczygiel.

"*Stabbed?* I didn't know that. That's a damned clumsy way to use a bayonet."

"You're an expert with that weapon," said Kennelly.

"I've had occasion to use it," said Hay.

"You cut throats with it," said Kennelly.

"Stabbing is a dumb way to kill a man," said Hay.

"Unless you pierce the heart, say, with the first penetration of the knife, he's apt to scream and struggle, maybe try to escape, maybe fight back. You can't just stick a knife in a man and watch him quietly fall down and die. It doesn't work that way."

"Cutting the throat is better," said Kennelly.

"A man with his throat cut doesn't yell. He can't. He's horrified. He knows he's dead. He doesn't struggle."

"Oh, Mr. Hay!" Mrs. Roosevelt protested.

"I'm sorry, Ma'am. I'm sorry, but these gentlemen are investigating a murder; and if they don't already know, they should be made aware of what a stabbing is like."

"I assume you heard and saw nothing," she said.

"I'd had a long day. That, plus the gin . . . I slept like a babe."

"We may have additional questions, Mr. Hay," said the First Lady. "In the meantime, thank you."

When Hay was gone and the door closed, Kennelly shook his head. "I don't believe him."

"I think we should take something into consideration," said Mrs. Roosevelt. "It has troubled me from the beginning."

"Ma'am?"

"If Mr. Hay, or someone else, murdered Officer Douglas then fled to the third floor—and slept in one of the guest rooms there—why did he leave a bed that had obviously been slept in, and leave damp towels? Why would he not carefully have made the bed and refrained from using towels and leaving them damp? Whoever spent the night in that room—and Mr. Hay says it was he—was at no pains to conceal the fact that he had been there."

"We'll figure it out," said Kennelly.

6

ONLY A FEW DAYS after his inauguration, President Roosevelt had paid a personal call on retired justice Oliver Wendell Holmes. It was remarked on as a most unusual thing for a president of the United States to call on a citizen at his home, particularly President Roosevelt, who did not move easily from place to place.

Now, on this evening in May, the president came to see Justice Holmes again. The first visit had been a surprise. This one was not. The old gentleman, with ninety-two years behind him, was expecting the call and was dressed for it, in the formal style of the past century, complete with swallowtail coat. He stood before his fireplace, now filled with yellow flowers, and nodded gently as this new president approached him, propelling himself across the room in his wheelchair.

Justice Holmes's great white mustache wobbled as he nodded and said, "I am honored, Mr. President."

"It is I who am honored, Mr. Justice."

"Well . . . Be seated all," said Holmes.

Mrs. Roosevelt had come from the White House, though in a separate car, since she would be going on to a dinner later. The president had been accompanied by

Dean Acheson and Professor Rexford Tugwell, the expert on farm economics. Felix Frankfurter was there at Holmes's invitation. He had been a law clerk to Justice Holmes and was now a professor of law at Harvard. He was a guest in the Holmes house.

"We brought you a little gift," said the president. "Do the honors, will you, Dean?"

Acheson unwrapped an insulated box and showed the justice half a dozen bottles of fine champagne.

"Ah!" said Holmes. "Uh . . . not from a bootlegger, I trust."

"A gift to the White House from the French ambassador," said President Roosevelt.

"Good! I never deal with bootleggers."

"Which makes it somewhat difficult to get your supplies, doesn't it, Mr. Justice?" Frankfurter commented.

Holmes smiled. "I don't put too fine a point on it," he said. "What you bring me, boy, I drink. I accept whatever explanation you give me as to its origin."

Oliver Wendell Holmes, Junior, was the son of Oliver Wendell Holmes the Boston physician, poet, and essayist, who wrote "The Wonderful One-Hoss Shay" and "Old Ironsides" ("Aye, tear her tattered ensign down . . ."). His son graduated from Harvard as the father had done and served three years as an officer in a Massachusetts regiment, fighting in such battles as Antietam, where he was wounded. He taught law at Harvard and resigned to serve on the Massachusetts Supreme Court. In 1902, President Theodore Roosevelt appointed him to the U.S. Supreme

Court, where he served until 1932. He was generally regarded as the finest mind on the Court during those years.

He retired from the Court after he found himself dozing off during arguments. Until his most recent years, he never missed a new show at the Gayety Burlesque. Every day, now, he was driven around Washington, to look at and remember the city where he had lived more than thirty years.

The champagne was poured. "I have always enjoyed fizzle water," said the old man as the effervescence of the champagne dampened his mustache.

"How do you like our new programs by now?" asked the president.

"You seem to have taken to heart what I told you when you came to see me in March. Remember what I said? 'Form your ranks . . . and *charge!*' You have done that." The justice shrugged. "But sometimes a charge breaks against a line and is driven back."

"We—"

The president's response was interrupted by the arrival of Justice Louis D. Brandeis. Brandeis was the second member of the famous Holmes-Brandeis dissenters, who had challenged the conventional wisdom of the conservative Supreme Court repeatedly in the 1920s.

"You're late, Louie," said Holmes.

"Is it too much to ask of a lawyer," Brandeis asked wryly, "that he write a brief so that, if you didn't check the cover page, you could tell which side of the case he was arguing? And I have to read all that malarkey."

"Well . . . have some fizzle water. That will ease your mind."

Having stood to greet Justice Brandeis, Mrs. Roosevelt returned to her seat beside Professor Frankfurter.

They had known each other since 1918, when Assistant Secretary of the Navy Franklin Roosevelt had brought him home to dinner at their home in Washington. "A fascinating man," she had written at the time, "but very Jew." She had quickly overcome that bias—which had been inevitable for her in the society in which she had lived—and had become a close friend of Frankfurter.

They had been talking about the Jews in Germany, and Frankfurter resumed the conversation—

"It's worse than anyone here can imagine," he said. "I received a letter from a friend in Stuttgart who says that his shoe shop was burned out, simply burned to the ground while the firemen played their hoses on nearby buildings to prevent sparks from spreading the fire and put no water on his store. Storm troopers stood around and laughed."

"I've heard of such things," said the First Lady.

"Mistreatment of women and girls is another thing," said Frankfurter. "Did you ever hear of Sara Lasky? She's a well-known ballerina, trained at the Bolshoi in Moscow. She was summoned before the *gauleiter* of Leipzig—meaning the city's party leader—and ordered to dance naked at a dinner he held for party bigwigs and certain industrialists."

"These are distressing things," said Mrs. Roosevelt. "Frank knows about them, but he's not sure what he can do about it."

"Something worse is coming. Hitler is going to rearm Germany. He's going to renounce the Treaty of Versailles and rearm."

"I should think Herr Hitler will be restrained by President von Hindenburg."

"Paul von Hindenburg is eighty-six years old, Eleanor."

She smiled and nodded at Justice Holmes. "He's ninety-two."

"Neither of those men have long," said Frankfurter grimly.

VII

1

THOUGH HE REMAINED CONVINCED that Ben Hay either had killed Douglas Douglas or had something to do with it, Ed Kennelly was a thorough cop, who believed in checking out all leads.

The name Angela Patchen, too, did not appear in the log when it should have. Kennelly decided it was worthwhile to give that a little attention. He talked with Szczygiel.

"There *is* something about Angela that troubles me a little," said Szczygiel. "Mrs. Roosevelt and I asked her a few questions, as you know. She said she didn't know the officer who was on duty at the security desk at the entrance to the Executive Wing. The duty roster showed that the officer on duty that evening was Frank Slye. I talked to him. He said Angela was 'a pleasant girl'—and that, even apart from her figure. He said she always had 'a cheery word or two.' That suggests to me that she did in fact know him."

"Suggests she's lying," said Kennelly.

"On the other hand," said Szczygiel, "Officer Harrigan, the man on duty at the west gate, confirms that she did leave in a cab at the time when she says she did." He grinned. "I suppose she could have climbed out a window."

"I have no doubt," said Kennelly dryly. "But *why?* Why would she do that?"

2

KENNELLY DECIDED TO CONFRONT this Angela Patchen. She had lied in a murder investigation, and that made it his business.

Like many government girls, she lived in a boardinghouse. When he arrived, at dusk, she was sitting on the front porch with three other young women.

"Angela Patchen?"

"I'm Angela."

"Lieutenant Edward Kennelly, D.C. police, Homicide Division. I'd appreciate it if you'd walk out to my car with me, where we can talk in private."

"Are you arresting me?"

"No. I just want to talk with you for a few minutes."

She glanced at the other girls, shrugged, and got up and went down the porch steps with him.

"Relax," he said when she was seated in the front seat of his unmarked Ford. "Cigarette?"

She nodded, and he shook two cigarettes from his package of Luckies and lit them with a kitchen match.

"When you talked with Stan Szczygiel and Mrs. Roosevelt, you did not tell the truth entirely," he said.

"What did I say that wasn't the truth?"

"You know. I'm not so much interested in the lie as in why you told it."

She blew a stream of smoke. "I don't have to talk to you," she said. "I don't have to let you question me. Just what authority you have over me?"

"Let's fix an understanding of what authority I have and whether you have to talk to me," said Kennelly firmly. "You're not under arrest, but you might be shortly."

He opened the glove compartment under the dashboard and pulled out a pair of handcuffs. Before she realized what was happening and could resist, he locked them on her wrists.

"Hey! What right you got to do this to me?" She shook her arms and jerked on the links between the cuffs. "What authority you got? How can you—?"

"Settle down, Angela," he said. "In the next five minutes you are going to be on your way to jail, or you are not. You can cooperate or not. Have it your way."

"I haven't done anything . . ." she sobbed. "Why do you want to treat me like this?"

"On Friday evening—the evening you did or did not

leave the West Wing by going past the security desk—a White House officer was stabbed to death. Murdered. That's why you are being questioned by a homicide detective."

"I swear before God, Sir," she murmured. "I didn't have anything to do with that. I've heard . . . a rumor that the man is dead. I know I haven't seen Officer Douglas around, when I used to see him all the time. Is he the one?"

"He's the one. We're keeping the matter confidential. If you want to be sure to spend some time in a cell down at headquarters, you just leak the story."

She lifted her hands and took a drag on her cigarette. "I couldn't leak anything. I don't *know* anything." She held her handcuffs in front of her face and frowned over them. "Why these?" she asked. "Honest to God, why these?"

"You said you wouldn't talk to me. Well, you are going to. You said I didn't have any authority over you. Well, I do. I just figured we'd establish that."

"They don't hurt," she said thoughtfully. "They're . . . humiliating." She blew smoke. "Hey! Am I a *suspect* in this murder?"

"I'd rather call you a witness."

"Okay. I didn't see anything. I didn't hear anything. I wasn't anyplace near where Doug was murdered."

"Where was he murdered?"

She shook her head and burlesqued a smile. "You can't trap me that way," she said. "Ask around about the rumor. The rumor is that Doug was killed in the main house, on the second floor."

"You were on a first-name basis with him?"

"I'm on a first-name basis with just about every guy I meet, Lieutenant. I bet I will be with you, shortly. They eye my knockers, and I'm Angela or Angie, no more Miss Patchen."

"How about Frank Slye? You know him?"

"Sure."

"Well, he was on duty at the security desk when you went past and didn't get noted in the log."

"*Frank!* Frank . . . ? He—well, okay. Look." She pulled up her skirt, showing the tops of her stockings and her bare legs above, plus the straps of her garters. "He asked me to show him my legs. He often did, if we were alone. So I did it, just like this. Then he begged me to let him have a look at my . . . you know what. I guess he got distracted—so distracted he didn't write in the log."

"You ever let a man see?"

"You asking, Lieutenant? I'll make you a deal. You take the cuffs off, I'll take my blouse and brassiere off."

"Tempting," he said. "But I'm an old Irish cop. And married. And a father. The question was, do you ever let any of the White House officers see you?"

"No. Well . . . not on duty. Not in the White House. I've dated a couple of White House cops over the years. And one Secret Service agent." She pushed down her skirt. "I get no end of propositions. You wouldn't believe it."

"I believe it. Ever think of marrying?"

"I've seen enough of marriage to know I'll never do it," she scoffed. "My parents . . . my sisters. How's the old saying go? 'Keep 'em pregnant in the winter and barefoot in the summer.' Not me."

"You're father is in the trucking business, I believe," he said.

Angela grinned. "You believe that?" she sneered. "Ha! You can find out from the Columbus police or the Franklin County sheriff easy enough. My father is a *bootlegger!* He was a brewer and a damned good one, until the bluenoses got their Prohibition through. He's made beer all these years. The cops don't care. When the Prohibition agents come through, the cops swear there's no brewery in Columbus. Well . . . See how long it takes my old man to start shipping legal beer again, once Repeal is in place."

"I understand there's more money in illegal beer than in legal," said Kennelly.

"We'll find out," she said. She flipped her cigarette out the window. "Wanta give me another one?" she asked. She was calm. The handcuffs didn't seem to bother her any longer. She accepted another Lucky and a light. "I could have gone into his business," she said. "I figured I'd wind up in jail. I figured he would. I didn't realize how much political pull he had."

Kennelly lit another cigarette for himself. "Ever think of going back to Columbus?" he asked.

"No. People in this part of the country think it's a hick

town. It's nowhere near as hick as Washington. Washington . . . Well, I was thinking of moving on, not back home but maybe to New York. But Washington has got exciting since the New Deal moved in. If I were going to marry . . . give me one of those bright young lawyers from Harvard. We could live in New York. That's where I wanta be."

"I'll take your cuffs off now, Angela. And you can go back up on the porch."

"Thanks, Ed."

He smiled faintly. "You haven't told me the truth, entirely, even now. But I'll let it go for the moment. Think about it, Angela. How *did* you get out of the West Wing Friday night? And why not the regular way? You want to make sure you've got no trouble, you can answer those questions."

"I have—"

"No you haven't," he interrupted firmly. "And let me tell you something more. I'm investigating a murder. If you were involved Friday night in something stupid, something that would get you in trouble but wasn't a big crime, you can tell me, and I don't have to report it to anybody. Keep that in mind."

Angela rubbed her wrists. "Thanks, Ed," she said softly.

3

KENNELLY HAD CHECKED THE personnel file on Frank Slye and drove from Angela's boardinghouse to the boardinghouse where Slye lived. The man was divorced. He lived in a room in a big house only eight blocks from where Angela lived.

Boardinghouses were strictly segregated by sex, and this one was for men. He found a male version of the scene in front of Angela's women's boardinghouse: men sitting on the porch on a warm spring evening, smoking pipes and cigars and chatting.

"This here Ruzey-velt's got her all wrong," he heard one man say as he came up the walk.

"Good evening, gents. Is Frank Slye around?"

"No. Not right now, Sir. I wouldn't be surprised you could find him at the Farragut Club. He favors the place."

Kennelly knew the Farragut Club very well. It was a speakeasy, as honest as a speakeasy ever got. He favored it himself and occasionally went in for a drink.

The man at the door recognized him and let him in without asking to see a membership card. Kennelly saw, though, that the man picked up a telephone. Without doubt he was reporting the entry of Lieutenant Kennelly of the D.C. police.

"Hi, Ed," said Sam Wenzel, the proprietor. "Welcome."

The Farragut was very different from what it had been before Prohibition. It had been an old-fashioned saloon, serving tankards of beer and offering free lunch, its floors covered with sawdust. Now it was a cocktail lounge, serving mixed drinks to a fashionable crowd. The floor was clean and polished. Wenzel wore a tux, as did many of the men at the bar and at the tables. The old crowd, who had drunk beer and eaten the free pretzels and baloney, couldn't afford the place anymore.

Although the Farragut had never been raided, it was equipped to be. If the alarm sounded, the men at the bar would dump their drinks into a zinc trough where water would have begun to gush. Men at the tables would rush to pour their drinks into the trough. The running water would sluice every trace of alcohol down the drains in half a minute. The bartenders would shove all the bottles through the doors behind them, into carts that would move quickly to haul the liquor to the cellar and into hidden pits under the floor.

Prohibition goons would find a wet trough, bottles of ginger ale, and men and women demurely drinking that and seltzer water.

Sam was sick of the whole deal and had promised Kennelly he would convert the Farragut back into a saloon the day after Repeal.

"I'm looking for Frank Slye."

"Right over there," Sam said, nodding toward a man a little way down the bar. "The one smoking a pipe."

Kennelly moved up beside Slye. "Lieutenant Kennelly," he said. "D.C. Homicide."

Slye nodded. "I know. Brought in to work on the case of Doug Douglas."

"Yes. Exactly. You were on duty at the security desk at the door to the West Wing, right?"

"From four to twelve," said Slye.

A bartender put a glass of Scotch in front of Kennelly, with a glass of water.

"Angela Patchen."

"Stan Szczygiel asked me about her."

"I guess you are absolutely certain she did not pass your desk that evening."

"I'm absolutely certain. Absolutely. She's not the kind of girl you'd overlook."

Kennelly sipped whiskey. "Okay. Let me tell you *her* story," he said. "She says you asked her to pull up her skirt and show you her legs—which she says you did before—and that she did it. She says that must have distracted you so much that you forgot to write her name in the log."

Slye smiled sarcastically. "Do you believe that?"

"No, I don't believe it. What I'd like to know is why she goes to such trouble, takes such a risk, to hide the fact that she did not leave the West Wing the way she says she did. What in the hell was she trying to do?"

"She could not have climbed out a window, I don't think," said Slye. "She could not have gone out through the double doors in the Oval Office. There were too many people still at work in the West Wing at that time of the evening for her to move around unseen. I'd guess she didn't leave at all, that she was still in the West Wing until after midnight and maybe all night."

"Doing what?"

"Well . . . Going through someone's files, let's say."

"Let's say. But looking for what? What does the girl have going on the side?"

Slye shrugged. He looked quizzical as the bartender put a fresh mug of beer in front of him. He had not ordered it and probably understood that it was a gift to Ed Kennelly.

"She took a hell of a risk," said Kennelly. "The gate guard confirms that she left by taxi. The only hole in her story is that you won't confirm that she came past your desk."

"Not won't. Can't."

"Why did she think you would?"

"Well—" He lifted his mug and took a taste of his new beer. "—I can only say that she probably didn't expect me there. I was called in at the last minute, when McKay went to the hospital."

"Are you suggesting that she'd somehow set it up with McKay to enter her name in the log even when she didn't come past?"

"I'm not suggesting anything."

"But it's a possibility, isn't it?" Kennelly asked.

"I don't know McKay well, but I don't think she could get him to do that."

"What would you call her, Frank? A flirt? Or something worse?"

"Well . . . She's a minx. I don't know I could call her anything worse."

"Is she having an affair?"

"I wouldn't know."

"If you had to guess . . ."

"I guess I'd think about Bob Hogan. I've seen some pretty knowing glances go back and forth between them. Officer Robert Hogan."

4

WHEN SHE LEFT THE little party for Mr. Justice Holmes, she went to the Mayflower Hotel, where she arrived just as the dishes were being cleared after a dinner for the wives of Democratic members of the Senate and House. She had warned the sponsors that she would be necessarily late, and no one took offense. She was led to the dais and was introduced. She said a few words of greeting and sat down.

"We are honored by the presence of the First Lady," said the mistress of ceremonies. "We are honored also by another guest who has been with us for dinner and now will favor us with selections on the piano. Ladies and gentlemen, Mr. George Gershwin!"

Gershwin, who was thirty-five years old, had already created an oeuvre of which a classical composer might have been proud. Besides *Rhapsody in Blue* and *An American in Paris*, he had written the opera *Porgy and Bess* and the scores for such musicals as *Lady Be Good*,

Funny Face, and the political satire *Of Thee I Sing*, for which he won the Pulitzer Prize.

He began by playing the song that first made him famous—"Swanee"—and followed with more songs, including "The Man I Love," "I Got Rhythm," and "Someone to Watch Over Me." He concluded with selected piano parts from *An American in Paris* and *Rhapsody in Blue.*

The audience accorded him a standing ovation that went on for some minutes.

He smiled and bowed. Then he was led over to talk with Mrs. Roosevelt. They had been introduced as soon as she reached the dais, but now they would have time to exchange a few words.

"I am quite familiar with your work, Mr. Gershwin, and appreciate it enormously."

"I am familiar with yours, Mrs. Roosevelt, and appreciate *it* enormously," Gershwin said, showing the smile that was a prominent element of his personality.

"How very nice of you, Mr. Gershwin."

"I would like to send you some records."

"I should be most grateful to have them. But send them to the president. He does not get out much at night, you know, and loves to listen to records. He has a very fine machine and listens to music almost every evening."

"I will send some to each of you," said Gershwin.

"How very kind."

She had to take time to speak with congressional wives. One of them was Mrs. Carter Glass, wife of the crusty, outspoken senator from Virginia. Senator Glass had opposed the nomination of Franklin Roosevelt. He said he didn't like to see a man work so hard to win a nomination. In the Senate now, he was the leader in pushing through the New Deal programs in banking and securities reform. He was a liberal in that respect, but FDR called him "an unreconstructed rebel."

"Th' problem y' have with the Nigras," Mrs. Glass said to Mrs. Roosevelt, "is that y've had no *experience* with them. Y' get to know 'em, y'll take a very different attitude."

"In what way?" asked the First Lady.

"What y' do not understand is that the Nigras in Virginia, the ones I see an' know, have got to be just about the happiest people in the world. They dance an' sing an' play the banjo an' jus' have a jolly old time. They work at simple jobs that don't make much demand on 'em. They don't waste their energy tryin' to do things that are beyond them. They got no worries. None at all. They leave it to *us* to do the worryin'."

"I'm glad to hear it," said Mrs. Roosevelt.

"You ought to come and see them perform," said Mrs. Glass. "It's such *fun* to see them sing and dance—

Weel a-bout and turn a-bout
And do just so.
Every time I weel a-bout
I jump Jim Crow."

"Jim Crow laws are—" Mrs. Roosevelt began.

"*Come see!* They don't care about Jim Crow laws. They don't *know* about Jim Crow laws. To the Nigra it's a song and dance."

"I appreciate your informing me about this," said Mrs. Roosevelt.

VIII

1

THE PRESIDENT AND MISSY had watched a movie after he returned from his visit with Holmes: *Grand Hotel*, with Greta Garbo, Joan Crawford, John Barrymore, and Wallace Beery. They had seen it before but thought it worth seeing again. After the picture, she put on some records.

The president, in his pajamas, sat propped against fluffed-up pillows, a Camel in the holder atilt in his mouth. Missy, in a royal-blue silk nightgown covered by a sheer white peignoir, sipped from the last glass of the bottle of red wine they had shared. It was a peaceful time and a good end to the day.

But then the telephone rang.

Missy answered. "What? *You!* How *dare* you call me here? How'd you get the switchboard to put you through? This is *outrageous!* I don't want to talk to you anytime. But to talk to you now, and *here . . . !* How'd you know where I am, anyway? Don't you ever dare do this again! You hear me? Not ever!"

Missy hung up. Immediately she began to tap the plunger to raise the White House operator. "Yes. The president's room. Why did you put that call through?" *** "He said he was *who?*" *** *"Damn!"*

The president had never seen Missy angry. "What's up?" he asked.

"That . . . *creep* told the operator he was J. Edgar Hoover and said he had to talk to the president, urgently."

"Who is the creep?" asked the president.

"His name is Nathan Clarke. He thinks he's got a crush on me. He's from New York. I met him during the nineteen-twenty campaign. He's got money he hasn't even counted yet. He proposed marriage right off—that is, in nineteen-twenty. He said he'd take me around the world, that we'd live on his yacht, and so on. It was all very appealing, but I didn't like him; besides which, I didn't trust him. So he married another woman. She divorced him, and he called me and proposed again. By then we were living in the governor's mansion in Albany. Again I turned him down. He's bothered me from time to time, and lately he's gotten persistent. He's going to marry me and take me away from all this."

The president took his cigarette holder from his mouth and showed the big, toothy Roosevelt smile. "I don't know. Maybe you ought to think about it. Going off to live on a yacht . . . Living like a queen . . . Cruising . . . Spending . . ."

"Effdee," Missy said solemnly, not at all amused. "If you're suggesting I should consider a thing like that, maybe I *should* consider it."

"My earnest prayer would be that you would consider it and reject it. I have no right to demand that you stay and burden yourself with the load that goes with this work. But I would miss you. I would surely miss you."

She nodded and smiled. "You know I won't leave, Effdee," she murmured.

"I know. I am deeply grateful."

"*I* am grateful," she said.

"Well, then. That telephone call is a serious criminal offense. Shall I—?"

"No. It would be embarrassing. I'd rather forget it."

"It seems somehow I should remember this man."

"He worked on the nineteen-twenty campaign. He gave a lot of money. He thinks you *should* remember him."

The president shook his head. "I can't place him. I can't place a face with the name."

"He thinks that being wealthy justifies him in anything he wants to do. There might be a bit of justification if he'd earned the money. But he didn't. He inherited it."

"If he doesn't take heed from the way you talked to him, you may have to bring the law against him."

2

AT KENNELLY'S REQUEST, SZCZYGIEL pulled the personnel file on Officer Robert Hogan.

Hogan, Robert T.

255 G Street, N.W.

B. Washington, 11 July 1899, son of Robert W. Hogan and Mary McCartney.

Married 1924, Imelda Ramos (Philippines). Son, daughter.

Enlisted United States Marine Corps 1917. Participated in Meuse-Argonne Campaign. Bronze Star, 1918. Assigned, 1919, to Marine contingent on U.S. gunboat *Panay,* cruising Yangtze River in China. Promoted to private first class 1917, corporal 1919, sergeant 1921, staff sergeant 1923, gunnery sergeant 1925. Honorable discharge 1925.

Applied, appointed White House police, 1925. Ratings and reports: excellent to good.

ADDENDUM: <u>CONFIDENTIAL</u>

Officer Hogan has a reputation for being something of a ladies' man, in spite of the fact that he is married and the father of two. A complaint against him, made by a secretary in the Executive Wing, was resolved without action, except a private warning. Officer Hogan denied the allegations made against him. Another secretary was transferred to the Treasury Department on complaint by her supervisor that she was neglecting her work to make occasion for clandestine meetings with Officer Hogan.

No suggestion of any problems of this nature has been made by any of Officer Hogan's supervisors.

"So little Angela," said Kennelly. "I wonder if she knows Hogan."

3

GENERAL DOUGLAS MACARTHUR, ARMY chief of staff, was first on the president's schedule of visitors that Tuesday morning. As always, the subject for discussion was the military budget, which the president was proposing to cut. It was the largest item in the nation's budget, and the president felt the armed forces should not be exempt from those sacrifices other departments of government were being asked to make.

MacArthur had a flair for the melodramatic. "My only

hope," he pronounced in his deep, stagey voice, "is that when some young American soldier is dying from a bayonet wound in his belly, after a military debacle occasioned by this country's lack of necessary arms, his dying words will be a curse, not mentioning the name MacArthur but using the name Roosevelt."

The president flared. "You can't talk that way to the president of the United States."

MacArthur stood. "Sir, you have my resignation," he said curtly and turned to walk toward the door.

"Don't be a fool, Douglas," the president said. "There's nothing that can't be worked out between reasonable men."

MacArthur drew and exhaled a deep breath. He returned to his chair. "I apologize for my intemperate remark," he said.

"You feel strongly," said the president. "You *should* feel strongly. Any disagreements between us are professional, not personal."

4

STAN SZCZYGIEL MADE A routine morning check of the logs at the security desks and gatehouses.

"Something odd," he said to Kennelly a little later when they sat down over coffee in his tiny office. "I saw General MacArthur walk out of the West Wing. He was noted in and out on the log at the desk there. But he was not logged in or out at the gates."

"So, he's got his own way in and out of the White House," said Kennelly. "I suppose, bein' chief of staff, he might have. You don't figure *he* killed—"

"No, no, of course not. But if *he* has a way into the White House, then somebody else could have."

"We can be damned sure he didn't come in through the rainwater tunnels. Not him, in his dashing uniform and varnished boots."

"He didn't come in that way," Szczygiel agreed. "I can think of one other way. If he has the key, he can come in through the tunnel from the Treasury Building. But *General MacArthur . . . !*"

"He's not as squeaky clean as you might think," said Kennelly. "In police work we come across some odd things from time to time."

"Like what?"

"He keeps a mistress in a suite in the Hotel Chastleton. She's Eurasian and beautiful beyond all belief. Her name is Isabel Cooper. She's the daughter of a Chinese woman and a Scottish father. The general brought her here from the Far East."

"But he lives—"

"He lives with his aged mother in the chief-of-staff's mansion at Fort Myer," said Kennelly. "She doesn't know about Isabel."

"Which means . . . ?"

"The general is a mama's boy," said Kennelly. "He'd

do anything to prevent mama from finding out about Isabel—which means he is subject to blackmail."

"Oh, come on!"

Kennelly shrugged. "Many and many a case has turned on just that."

"Well . . . Are you going to investigate General MacArthur?"

"Very discreetly," said Kennelly.

5

HE DECIDED TO BE a good deal less than discreet in his investigation of Ben Hay. Knowing that Hay was at work in the Executive Wing, Kennelly went to his apartment, which was in a brown brick building on 16th Street.

One of his skills as an investigator was opening locks. He carried with him a ring of skeleton keys, plus a pick, should he need it. He didn't need it. The simple lock yielded to one of the keys on the ring, and Kennelly walked in.

Hay lived well, obviously not on the salary of a government lawyer. He had a large living room with a dining alcove, a kitchen, a bedroom, and a bathroom.

He had a living-room set, consisting of a davenport that obviously folded out to make a bed, a deep wing chair, and a matching wing chair on rockers. They were upholstered with mohair: taupe with rose background. At the end of the living room sat a small mahogany roll-top desk. Between the windows was a radio console on turned legs, closed now to hide the knobs and dial of the instrument.

In the dining room sat a Queen Anne–style table of fumed oak with two chairs in the same style, upholstered with leather.

The oak floors were covered by two rugs, a large one in the living room and a small one in the dining alcove. They were dark tan with flowers and foliage in dark red and green.

Four wrought-iron floor lamps with fluted shades would light the room at night.

It was completely middle class: comfortable but unimaginative. Except for one thing. Hanging on the wall above the couch was a large painting that was wholly incongruous with everything else in the room. It was of four nude or seminude people, a man and three women, powerfully rendered, he supposed, but absolutely unrealistic. The naked man was playing a violin. Two seminude women were dancing. A nude woman sat and listened.

Kennelly squinted at the black signature: Henri·Matisse He knew little about art, but he recognized the name as that of a famous French artist, and he guessed the painting had been hugely expensive.

Kennelly went to the desk and rolled back the top. The pigeonholes were stuffed with papers. Methodically, he pulled out the contents of each one separately, scanned the papers, and put them back in the same order in which he found them.

At first he found nothing of interest. Then—

```
April 13, 1933
Dear Ben,
This is just a note to remind you of
your obligation to us. We don't mean to
press, but it would be nice if you gave
us some word about what we can expect.
                    Yours very truly,
                    AB for AF
```

O.K. 4/24/33

Kennelly had no warrant, of course, and he could not carry away anything from the apartment. He wished he had a camera and could photograph the note.

In another cubbyhole he found a receipt from a New York jewelry store—

MISTRAL CUSTOM JEWELERS
FINEST QUALITY JEWELRY AND WATCHES
345 MADISON AVENUE
NEW YORK, NEW YORK

SOLD TO: ***Mr. Benjamin Hay, City***
One ladies platinum ring set with 1 1/2 ct. diamond
$915.25, sales tax incl
–$75.00 discount for cash

–$40.25 good will
Received $800 Paid in full
February 11, 1933.
Thank you! Thos. Mistral

Eight hundred dollars was three times what Ben Hay was paid per month as a lawyer in the White House. Some lady had been treated very generously.

Kennelly moved on to the bedroom. It was furnished like the living room, with a comfortable, mundane canopied bed, two matching walnut nightstands, and an immense faux-antique mahogany bureau.

He learned very quickly that a woman shared the apartment with Ben Hay. He found her clothes in the bureau and in the closet. He was no judge of women's clothes, but he recognized in what he saw the flair of a woman of expensive tastes. She did not wear bloomers but instead wore tap pants, the skimpy, flimsy garments that barely covered a woman's bottom and left her legs bare from the hips down. Hers were not rayon, as most were, but were silk. She wore sheer silk stockings, sometimes apparently with garters that hung from a belt, other times rolled over garters just above her knees. Her dresses and blouses, hanging in her closets, were also chiefly silk, though he recognized some sweaters as cashmere and some skirts as Scottish wool.

Beneath the woman's underwear in the second drawer of the bureau lay a tooled-leather jewel box, supposedly concealed, bearing the initials *JP*. It did not contain a one-and-a-half carat diamond ring, but it contained other rings, plus bracelets and necklaces—none costume jewelry, none cheap.

In the bathroom, a razor and shaving cup sat on the rim of the sink. The cabinet was filled with cosmetics: lipsticks in several shades, mascara, rouge, and eye shadow in several colors. If the woman had dark-brown hair, the color was deepened and evened by something called Walnutta.

In the drawer of one of the nightstands, a supply of cockrubbers proved the friendship here was not platonic.

Kennelly would have liked to search further in the cubbyholes of the desk to try to learn the identity of the woman who lived here. He realized, though, that he did not have the time. Hay would be at the White House until evening. The woman might return at any time. He looked around and satisfied himself he had not left any evidence of his intrusion. Then he decamped.

It may have been well that he did. As he was starting his car, he noticed a V-12 Lincoln pull to the curb. A woman with dark-brown hair got out and, all elegance and composure, strode across the walk and into the brown-brick apartment building.

Was she the one living with Hay? Kennelly would have liked to know.

6

"THE FACT THAT MR. Hay lives beyond what would seem to be his means is suggestive," said Mrs. Roosevelt. "It proves little."

They sat in her study. Once more she had put aside her scruples and arranged for Kennelly and Szczygiel to have Scotch and gin in late afternoon.

"It suggests motive," said Ed Kennelly. "How much money would somebody pay a man to assassinate the president?"

"I will make a contact in New York and try to discover just how much Mr. Hay may be worth," said the First Lady. "It may be a great deal more than we suspect. After all, we don't know how much he may have inherited."

"I am reluctant to mention it," said Stan Szczygiel, "but we took notice this morning that General MacArthur seems to have a key to the Treasury Building tunnel."

Mrs. Roosevelt grinned. "You're not suggesting that General MacArthur—?"

"No. No. Not at all," said Szczygiel. "But—"

"The general is subject to blackmail," said Kennelly. "He brought a beautiful Eurasian girl home when he returned from the Far East. Her name is Isabel Cooper. He keeps her in a suite in the Hotel Chastleton. He—"

"I am afraid arrangements like that are altogether too prevalent," said the First Lady. "I can't imagine the general could be blackmailed over it. After all, he is a single man."

"But his mother doesn't know about it, and General MacArthur is altogether a mama's boy," said Kennelly.

"Well . . ." mused Mrs. Roosevelt. "His mother—she is called Pinky, I believe—came to the town of West Point when Douglas came to the military academy. She lived in Craney's Hotel all four years of his time at West Point."

"I think there is a remote possibility—very remote, I acknowledge—that someone weaseled a key, or a copy, out of the general by threatening to expose his relationship with Isabel."

"Another question," said Mrs. Roosevelt. "Maintaining a mistress in a hotel suite must be very expensive. Has the general a fortune? If so, where did he get it?"

"A very good question," said Kennelly.

"All this is quite fanciful," she said. "If you pursue this line of inquiry, you must be very discreet."

"I am not finished with Angela," said Szczygiel.

7

OFFICER ROBERT HOGAN WAS on duty in the West Wing. He did not man security desks but walked a beat in the wing, sometimes in the main house. Szczygiel found him and invited him into an office across the hall from the Cabinet Room. It was Tugwell's office, but Tugwell was in New York making a speech.

"I want to talk about Friday night," said Szczygiel.

Hogan nodded. "A tragedy," he said.

"Murder," said Szczygiel.

Hogan was beefy. His face was strong and square. He had oddly red cheeks. He wore his hair cut bristle-short, a style probably imposed on him during his eight years in the U.S. Marine Corps. Szczygiel had read his personnel file and knew that Hogan had served aboard the gunboat *Panay*, operating on the Yangtze River. He had attained the rank of gunnery sergeant. With that rank he might have been expected to make a career of the Corps. But he hadn't. He married a Filipino girl, left the Marines, and, being a Washingtonian, came home and applied for a job with the White House uniformed police. He seemed to have a talent for winning promotion; only seven years after joining the force, he was a sergeant.

"You were on duty Friday night."

"Yes *** Sir, four to midnight."

Hogan did not say, "Yes, Sir," as others did. Maybe it was a Marine habit to insert a pulse between *yes* and *sir* and to pronounce each word meticulously.

"You signed in at four and out at twelve."

"Yes *** Sir."

"Did Officer Slye sign you out?"

"Actually *** Sir, I signed myself out. I was making a last check and went to see how Officer Slye was doing at the security desk. He was most uncomfortable *** Sir. He needed to go to the bathroom. Normally I check duty stations every half hour or so, and often men ask me to take their station for five minutes while they go to the men's room. I told him to go ahead. It was ten till twelve, and I told him I'd hold his desk down that ten minutes and sign him out, so he could just leave. At the same time I signed myself out. Officer Gephart would take over at midnight. He was already in. I had seen him in the hall in the Executive Wing. I saw him coming, so I just went on. The desk was not left uncovered as much as half a minute."

"Miss Angela Patchen insists she signed out with Officer Slye, about half past seven. Her name is not on the log, and he insists she didn't. Do you have any explanation for that?"

"No *** Sir. Miss Patchen is an exceptionally interesting girl. I wouldn't want to try to guess what went on between her and Slye."

"Were you surprised to find Slye on duty?"

"Yes *** Sir. Officer McKay had that duty. I found out later that he had been rushed to the hospital for an emergency appendectomy."

IX

1

IT WAS HICK'S LAST night in Washington. She had to go back to New York, from where she would travel to the Midwest to report on farm conditions in states like Oklahoma and Kansas.

Mrs. Roosevelt was committed to visit the display of airplanes set up on the Mall. At that time of year, early evening would remain broad daylight, and crowds gathered to see the airplanes that had been hauled in, some of them disassembled and reassembled, for public view.

It was understood, too, that on this evening celebrities would be present. Of them, for this crowd, the First Lady would not be the most interesting.

Mrs. Roosevelt wore a white frock and a broad-brimmed white straw hat. The horsy Lorena Hickock wore a nondescript yellow dress.

A Mr. Litchfield, director of the show, greeted the

First Lady and offered to escort her and her friend to the most interesting exhibits.

"I've flown in one of those," said Hick, pointing to a Ford Tri-Motor marked with the insignia of United Airlines.

"Flying is an intriguing experience," said the First Lady. "Amelia Earhart flew me from New York to Baltimore in March. She instructed me carefully in how to open my parachute, but I'm not certain I could have done it. Can you imagine having to leave your airplane hundreds of feet in the air? There you would be. I am not certain I could have retained the presence of mind to pull on the ring and release the chute. And I was dressed in flying clothes, all leather and straps, with a helmet and goggles, even though we were inside a closed plane. My!"

"I'm afraid my flight was nowhere near so adventuresome," said Hick. "The Tri-Motor seats twelve, all in ordinary clothes. The seats are wicker. You do have to wear a lap belt. They fly at about three thousand feet, at about one hundred and twenty-five miles an hour. I flew to Cleveland. You could look down and see you were passing fast trains on the New York Central."

"Yes. We did that. I believe Miss Earhart described our speed as exceeding one hundred miles an hour. She says airplanes will double that speed within a few years. Imagine that."

"The best part is the view," said Hick.

"Yes. Seeing the landscape go by under you is most fascinating," said Mrs. Roosevelt.

They walked around the Tri-Motor. It was powered by three radial engines, one under each wing, one in the nose. Passengers entered through a door on the right side, behind the wide wing. Two young women in navy-blue uniforms with short capes greeted people who wanted to climb up for a look inside.

"Those are the hostesses," Hick explained to the First Lady. "Each one has to be a registered nurse."

"That sounds ominous," said Mrs. Roosevelt.

"They try to be reassuring. They serve coffee and sandwiches. If anyone looks like he's about to upchuck, they're there with containers for it, plus stomach pills. Nobody had the problem on my flight, but I can't say I felt like eating."

"You'll find the GeeBee interesting, I'm sure," said Litchfield. "And Major Doolittle is here in person."

Policemen and Secret Service agents led Mrs. Roosevelt and Hick through a crowd and up to an airplane that was spectacular and unique. It was the notorious GeeBee, a racing plane known to be exceedingly difficult to fly.

Major Jimmy Doolittle was standing beside the yellow-and-black plane, talking to several men. When Litchfield approached with the First Lady, he told them he would talk with them later and turned his attention to her.

"An honor, Ma'am," he said.

"The honor is mine, Major Doolittle."

"Actually, Ma'am, I'm *Mister* Doolittle. I'd only made

lieutenant in the Army Air Corps, so I retired and joined the Shell Oil Company. Then the army made me a reserve major, but I'm a mister, really. And content to be so."

Mrs. Roosevelt stared up at the big plane. It was almost as tall as it was long, sitting squat on stubby landing gear enclosed in streamlined fairings.

"It seems too short and fat to fly," said Hick.

The GeeBee—the name came from the Granville Brothers, who manufactured the plane in Springfield, Massachusetts—was in fact thickset and conspicuously heavy. Its enclosed cockpit was faired into the fuselage nearer the tail than the nose. The short wings and little stabilizers and rudder looked too small to lift and control it.

The huge radial engine dwarfed the rest of the airplane.

"It has been described," said Doolittle, "as a little bitty plane designed to haul one great big engine up in the air. It's a Pratt and Whitney Wasp and develops eight hundred horsepower. When you're flying the GeeBee, you're flying an engine. The rest is almost surplusage."

"It is extremely dangerous, I've heard," said Hick. "It has been involved in some spectacular crashes."

"When it crashes, the speed makes the crash spectacular."

"Why do you fly it?"

"It's a beautiful machine," he said. "Nothing else in the air comes near it."

"You've set a speed record," said Mrs. Roosevelt.

"Yes, two hundred and ninety-two miles per hour over a measured course."

"Two hundred and—!"

"It's capable of a little more, I think."

The *Winnie Mae,* in which Wiley Post had flown around the world, was on display. Post was not there.

The First Lady was able to stroll around the show without much attention being paid her. Washington was already accustomed to her, and this crowd was not composed of people with political axes to grind.

Even so, as they walked away from the *Winnie Mae,* she heard a friendly greeting—

"Ah, Mrs. Roosevelt! A pleasure!"

She turned and fixed a quizzical smile on Ben Hay.

"Got away a little early this evening," he said cordially. "I won't trouble you. I just wanted to say hello. And to introduce my friend Miss Jo Pointer."

Mrs. Roosevelt's eye dropped involuntarily and immediately to the young woman's left hand, where she saw a diamond solitaire ring with a stone greater than a full carat. Looking up, she found herself staring into the face of an exceptionally handsome, solemn-eyed, dark-haired woman of maybe twenty-five years.

"I am honored, Mrs. Roosevelt."

"Well . . . I am pleased to meet you. And meet my friend Lorena Hickock."

"I have read some of your reports, Miss Hickock."

Hick nodded. She was flattered.

Jo Pointer was wearing a gray silk dress and no hat.

The dress fit her perfectly, clinging to her perhaps a little boldly, revealing that she was wearing nothing much under it.

"Do you fly, Miss Pointer?" asked Mrs. Roosevelt.

"From time to time. To and from Detroit."

"That's a very long flight," said Hick.

"Well . . . From New York."

"It's still a long flight. On the Tri-Motor?"

Jo Pointer smiled at Hay. "What else?"

2

HICK HAD CHOSEN A restaurant for their farewell dinner, one where they could have drinks and share a bottle of wine, which made the place a speakeasy. It was called Burkholder's. The First Lady of the United States was escorted to a back room, where she and Hick could dine alone—and Hick at least could drink—in privacy.

The specialty of the house was beer—very good beer, too, Hick said; and she insisted Mrs. Roosevelt try it. So foaming mugs were put before them.

"I am pleased to have met Miss Pointer," said the First Lady. "Messrs. Szczygiel and Kennelly are anxious to know who she is."

"What difference?" Hick asked.

"Well . . . She lives with Mr. Hay, in his apartment. She was wearing a diamond ring that he probably bought her, for nine hundred dollars. She was expensively dressed also. He has an original Matisse hanging in his living room. My investigators would like to know where he gets all that money."

"Well . . . I suppose I could look into it," said Hick. "I have a few days before I have to leave for the Midwest."

"In nineteen-thirty-one Mr. Hay was called by the district attorney to testify in a murder trial involving Mr. Arthur Flegenheimer—"

"Dutch Schultz."

"I believe he is so called. Mr. Hay was an alibi witness. It seems Mr. Flegenheimer and some of his friends testified that Mr. Flegenheimer was at a party at the time of the murder. Mr. Hay testified he was not. Also, it has been noted that other guests at that party were a Mr. Luciano, a Mr. Costello, and a Mr. Lansky."

"Jesus Christ! The top guys of the New York Mob. *The* top guys! Hay keeps nice company."

"The party was held at an establishment run by a certain Miss Adler, Miss Polly Adler."

"Polly's! She runs a high-class whorehouse!"

"Lieutenant Kennelly has a quaint name for it," said Mrs. Roosevelt with a smile. "He calls it a 'house of ill reputey.' "

"I should beg off the plight of Midwestern farmers and look into this story."

"Please don't, Hick dear. We are trying to be circumspect. It is essential that we be circumspect."

3

“A WILD-GOOSE CHASE,” said Stan Szczygiel.

“Probably,” said Ed Kennelly. “And got nothin’ to do with our problem. But you get a tip, you follow up the tip.”

“Your informant?”

“I let him stay out of jail, and he feeds me information. Routine police business.”

“I hear you guys let hookers work so you can make informants of ’em.”

“A hooker at work is worth six in the slammer,” said Kennelly.

“You let the Virginia cops know about this?”

“You kiddin’?”

“The FBI?”

“C’mon.”

“Well, Virginia is outside your jurisdiction.”

“But not beyond yours,” said Kennelly. “If we make an arrest, it’s yours. Only thing is, we’re not gonna make any arrests. I want to see what the hell’s going on.”

Kennelly knew where he was going and shortly pulled into the parking lot at the Clock. Ollie came to the door to greet him—

“Ed! You ol’ son of a gun! C’m in! C’m in! And Mr. . . . Trumble, as I recall.”

Kennelly grinned at Szczygiel. “You’ve been here before?”

"Once," said Szczygiel reticently. "I escorted a certain lady here."

"Well . . . Anyway, Ollie, it looks to me as if you're doing a hell of a lot better here than you did over in the District."

"You know me, Ed. I just work here. But you're right; it *is* a big improvement for me." He opened the door into the main room. "Some joint, huh?"

"Meyer Lansky?" asked Kennelly.

"Is that an official inquiry, or . . . ?"

"A social inquiry," said Kennelly.

"Well then, gents. This way."

He led them to a table near the wall and up front where they had a good view of the stage. A bored-looking girl was stripping, and about half the people in the speakeasy were watching her.

"Aimee Semple McPherson stripped here last week," said Szczygiel. "I wonder if—"

"She's working a joint at Saratoga," said Kennelly. "She's going back to Los Angeles in easy stages."

"You keep track of her?"

"At the request of the LAPD. They don't want her pulling another disappearing act and claiming again that she's been kidnapped. They'd love to be able to respond to reports of her kidnapping by saying, 'Oh, no, she's just stripping in Saratoga.' Every major police department in the country has a file on her."

Szczygiel glanced around the room. "J. Edgar Hoover and his boyfriend were here last week."

Kennelly glanced around. "Ah ha! Our informant was right. Look who's here."

Szczygiel looked where Kennelly's nod indicated, but he did not recognize the three men at a table in the middle and front of the room.

"There you are," said Kennelly. "That's Arthur Flegenheimer, otherwise known as Dutch Schultz. He's the one in the shabby suit. The dapper one is Dixie Davis, his lawyer. And the third one is the interesting one. That's Abbadabba Berman."

"A * * * bracadabra . . . ?"

"He's the mainstay of one of Dutch's most profitable lines of business. He's a mathematical genius—certifiable. He can glance at a string of figures and add them in his head in seconds. The numbers game in New York City is based on the handle at some racetrack, say Aqueduct. The Mob gets running reports on what numbers the suckers are betting. If somebody's hunch, rumored around, suggests a particular number, a lot of them bet that number. For example, all during March, there was heavy play on three hundred thirty-three—March 'thirty-three. Abbadabba watched the total play on the track tote board and told the gang what to bet so the final total would not end in three-three-three. I mean, they made sure that the final number wouldn't be five hundred forty-one thousand, three hundred thirty-three dollars, or some such number."

"Mathematical genius?" Szczygiel asked skeptically.

"Well, that's the simplest way to do it. Other games

are based on parimutuel numbers, which require a lot more sophistication to adjust."

"I've heard of Dutch Schultz," said Szczygiel.

"He's a beer baron," said Kennelly. "He's going to have to find a new racket when Prohibition ends."

Though he looked like an unsuccessful shoe salesman, Dutch Schultz apparently had a winning personality. He was all smiles. He even sent a beaming smile up to the girl on the stage, as if he appreciated her. He was engaged in animated conversation with his two companions.

Ollie came to the table. "Mr. Flegenheimer would like to buy you a bottle of champagne."

"How does he know who we are?" Kennelly asked sharply.

"Ed . . . I can't withhold information from a guy like that."

"You withheld it from me."

"I knew you'd recognize him as soon as you saw him."

"Who else is in the house that I should know?"

"Well . . . you ever hear of Bing Crosby . . . the singer? You see his movie last year? *The Big Broadcast.* Couldn't get any more popular than that."

"What's he doing here?"

"He's still chiefly, uh . . . a nightclub performer. He won't sing here. He sings where there'll be publicity. *You* know."

"So he's here to see the boss, I suppose," said Kennelly. "Meyer Lansky."

"Ed, c'mon! I can't talk about things like this."

"If he wants to make big money singing in clubs, he's got to keep on the right side of guys like Lansky," said Kennelly. "I understand a lot of performers do that. Jimmy Durante—"

"It doesn't mean they're part of the deal," said Ollie. " 'Cause they're not. But so long as the clubs that pay real money have got to be speakeasies, these guys have to—"

"Understood. Who's the woman? His wife?"

"You kiddin'? Glamour-puss is his girlfriend. She's just eighteen. He takes her everywhere—everywhere that he won't be seen."

"He's being seen here."

"Who's gonna admit he was here *to* see him?"

"Thanks, Ollie. Tell Mr. Flegenheimer we'll be glad to drink his champagne."

Stan Szczygiel shook his head. "I learn something new every day," he said.

"Which is what makes life worth living," said Kennelly. He raised a hand and waved a salute to Dutch Schultz.

The Dutchman grinned and returned the salute.

As Kennelly and Szczygiel sipped champagne and nibbled hors d'oeuvres, a couple came to Schultz's table. The three men there rose out of respect for the woman. They shook hands all around, and the man and woman sat down.

"Fancy that," said Szczygiel.

The man who had just sat down with the Dutchman was Ben Hay. With him was an exceptionally handsome woman in a gray silk dress.

"What I want to know is, who is she?" said Kennelly.

The conversation at the Dutchman's table caused everyone to turn and look at Kennelly and Szczygiel. Ben Hay pushed back his chair, rose, and came to their table.

"Gentlemen," he said. "How nice to see you."

"It's good to see you," said Kennelly. "I'm curious about something, though. You testified *against* Dutch Schultz. How is it that you two are friends?"

"Arthur is a perceptive and understanding man," said Hay. "He understood that I had been subpoenaed and that I didn't dare perjure myself. He never blamed me."

"Well, was he at the party or not?" asked Kennelly.

Hay glanced back at the other table. "He was not," he said simply.

"So he was guilty."

"That does not follow. Would you like to meet him? He would like to meet you."

"Why not?"

Hay led the two men to the other table. "Let me introduce Lieutenant Ed Kennelly of the D.C. police, Homicide Division, and Agent Stan Szczygiel of the Secret Service."

Schultz rose. "A pleasure," he said and introduced Davis and Berman. "And this is Miss Jo Pointer, Ben's friend."

Like Mrs. Roosevelt, Kennelly looked immediately to her left hand and saw the diamond. "Pointer . . ." he said. "I don't believe I know anyone else by that name."

"Check your files, Lieutenant," she said. She was pointedly acerbic but not unfriendly. "Here." She picked up a silver butter knife and squeezed it between two fingers. "There is a set of my fingerprints." She smiled. "Maybe you can identify me."

"I'm not particularly interested in identifying you, Miss Pointer. Only making conversation."

"Of course," she said smoothly. "Me, too."

"She's a great little gal," said the Dutchman. "A *great* little gal."

He spoke as if he were the most innocent man in the world, but Kennelly had to wonder why this meeting and what they were talking about.

"*I* appreciate her," said Hay.

"Well . . . We want to thank you for the champagne," said Kennelly.

"My pleasure," said Dutch Schultz.

Back at their table, Kennelly spoke to Szczygiel and said, "This raises more questions than it answers."

4

PASSING BY THE DOOR to the president's bedroom suite, Mrs. Roosevelt heard music and knew that the president was still awake. She also understood that Missy was with him. The president *could*, but only with painful effort, go to the player and change records.

She was grateful to Missy. She could not imagine herself sitting for an evening in the president's bedroom and changing records for him. While he was listening to music, he did not want to make conversation—which meant that she would have been sitting silent.

The First Lady went on to her own rooms. Tommy had left a stack of telephone notes for her, plus five letters for her signature. She scanned the notes, then reviewed and signed the letters, before she went to bed.

In the president's bedroom, Missy was playing records as Mrs. Roosevelt had supposed.

They had listened to show tunes, including songs from *Of Thee I Sing*, and now they were listening to one of the president's favorite pieces of music, Dvorak's *From the New World*.

The music ended. The president crushed out his final cigarette of the day.

"Tell me, girl," he said. "Has the creep bothered you today?"

"Yes. He called me this afternoon."

"We can tell the operator not to put his calls through."

"That will be difficult. He tells her he's somebody else. Today he was Joseph Kennedy."

"I wonder if he used the Boston accent."

"The poor operator put him through. He wanted to tell me how much more sparkling he can make life for me. He proposed marriage. He wants me to marry him aboard his yacht. He says he can bring it up Chesapeake Bay and moor off Annapolis, and he will invite you and Mrs. Roosevelt to be his guests. *Our* guests, as he puts it."

"Is he more than a nuisance?"

"He is a nuisance, Effdee, but I don't think more than that."

X

1

WEDNESDAY MORNING. A RAINSTORM had swept over Washington during the night and had not departed, leaving a steady cold drizzle.

Mrs. Roosevelt received a call from Missy, saying the president would like to see her in the Oval Office about nine. She went there. He sat behind the clutter of souvenirs and mementoes that covered the top of his desk. He had a fondness for clutter that the First Lady found a little distressing. He let his pince-nez drop from his nose and hang on its string. He pushed his chair back a little and lit another Camel.

"How far do you trust this fellow Szczygiel?" he asked. "I mean, do you trust him to be discreet? Absolutely discreet?"

"As much as I have ever trusted any man," she said.

The president winced. He was not sure if she was

giving him a dig about his old affair with Lucy Mercer, now so many years ago, or if she was simply stating a simple fact.

She saw his doubt and said, "Mr. Szczygiel is a trustworthy man."

"Very well. I speak to you and not directly to him because you know him well, whereas I hardly know him at all. I have an exceptionally delicate matter I would like him to look into. It must be kept a complete secret, from everyone but you and me—and him."

"I am sure Mr. Szczygiel is quite careful."

"Alright. Here's the problem. Missy is being harassed by a man who has a crush on her. It's not out of a clear blue sky. She's known him some thirteen years. He proposed marriage to her in nineteen-twenty, and she turned him down. He married another woman. They were divorced, and he proposed to Missy again. Again she turned him down. Now he calls her. And calls her. He even got a call through to my bedroom, where she was running a movie for me. He told the White House operator he was J. Edgar Hoover. Yesterday he got a call through to her office by saying he was Joe Kennedy."

"And you would like this stopped."

"Very, very discreetly. Missy must not know we intervened."

"I quite understand."

"The man is very wealthy. He wants to marry her on his yacht—with you and me as guests—and then take her cruising around the world. I daresay he has some influence. Brother Szczygiel must be more than careful."

2

LOOKING OUT THE WINDOW, toward the Ellipse and the Washington Monument, at the drizzle and remembering the hard rain during the night, Stan Szczygiel and Ed Kennelly reflected that the drainage tunnels must be full. Mrs. Roosevelt was not thinking of tunnels as they met in her study. They had coffee as usual, with some little pastries. It was her impression that these men often worked through their meal hours.

"I have to say that we seem to have made little progress," she said. "We have managed to keep the newspapers from learning of the cause of the death of Officer Douglas, but beyond that . . ."

"We have some suggestive evidence," said Kennelly. "One has to be patient with these things."

"I have a penchant," said the First Lady, "for organizing things graphically."

She had a blackboard standing on a sturdy tripod, and she took chalk from her desk and stepped up to the board.

"Now," she said. "We have Mr. Hay. And what do we know about him?"

She printed on the board—

MR. BENJAMIN HAY

PURPOSE: TO ASSASSINATE THE PRESIDENT?

ACCESS: YES.

MEANS: PROBABLY.

ASSOCIATES: OF QUESTIONABLE CHARACTER.

MOTIVE: ???

"What more do we know about Mr. Hay?"

"Add that he keeps an expensive girlfriend. Named Jo Pointer. It would be interesting to know who she is."

Mrs. Roosevelt added the information—

LADY FRIEND: MISS JO POINTER. WHO?

"Now," she said, "I believe we take some interest in the fact that Miss Angela Patchen did not sign out of the West Wing on Friday night, yet signed in from outside the next morning."

"Plus the fact that she clearly lied," said Szczygiel.

Mrs. Roosevelt wrote on the blackboard—

MISS ANGELA PATCHEN—FAILED TO SIGN OUT OF WEST WING.

PURPOSE: ???

ACCESS: POSSIBLE.

MEANS: ???

ASSOCIATES: VARIOUS. ATTRACTIVE GIRL. OFFICER HOGAN?

MOTIVE: ??? TO DO WHAT?

"That's not much," said Mrs. Roosevelt. "I have a sense that we are making no progress."

"I want to know," said Kennelly, "how it happens that Ben Hay is so close a friend of Dutch Schultz."

"Yes," said the First Lady. "But I should like to know what that has to do with a possible attempt to assassinate the president."

After Kennelly left, Mrs. Roosevelt spoke in strict confidence to Stan Szczygiel and told him about the president's request that he find out what he could about Nathan Clarke.

3

SOME OF HER CORRESPONDENCE was amusing, some distressing. Tommy picked out letters for her to read. Among those that Wednesday morning—

Dear Miz Ruseveldt,

Jesus is Lord. The Bible is the whole truth unerrant unchange the Word of God forever. We notice that you and your husban never mention Jesus the Lord or the truth of Scripcher in your talks and writes. You should tell the wurld the truth! Holy holy holy. You sin by silence. Pleese give us your insure that you beleeve. We wait your word.

Dear Mrs. Roosevelt,

The Cambridge Fellowship of Integral Socialists reviews with distaste your association with certain notorious counter-revolutionary reactionaries.

We cannot help but take note that the president's cabinet is packed with them. In a nation whose suffering people cry out for justice, it is intolerable that no true Marxist-Leninists are welcome at the seat of power.

Surely you are aware that your husband is only the American Kerensky and that true Revolution is no more than months away. It is inevitable. Marxism-Leninism is the future! Extend your friendship and cooperation to the Leninists of America and avoid the fate that befell the unhappy Nicholas II and his family.

We got no milc. We got no bred. Pleaze send $20. We will repay as soon as we can.

She would have liked to respond to the last letter, by sending a twenty-dollar bill. Unhappily, scores of such requests arrived daily. She could not even answer them, much less send the money desperately appealed for.

Other letters asked for work—jobs with the government—begging for assistance or citing services to the Democratic party or the Roosevelt campaign.

Some writers seemed to believe that the Roosevelts were benign despots who could override the laws and give whatever was asked. Some thought the Roosevelt family could alleviate the entire suffering of the unemployed from its own personal resources. Some despised the Roosevelts beyond any limit, accused them of all manner of crimes, and wished them ill.

For example—

> You goddam communist nigger lovers distroying our grate country. I praye night and day that Our Lord will strike you deef dumb and bline. Our famly <u>fought</u> for America while yer presdent pearsite sat on his but in Wash'ton and did nothing. Hell on you and all your kind!

4

STAN SZCZYGIEL DID NOT know quite what to do with the First Lady's request that he look into the background of Nathan Clarke. It was not what he was qualified to do. He knew very well he could not ask for help from the

FBI. Under the despotic rule of the egomaniacal Hoover, the federal bureau simply was not to be trusted with any information that might have political significance. Nothing would please Hoover more than to be able to open a file and insert some gossip about the president's private and confidential secretary.

On the other hand, Szczygiel believed he could trust Ed Kennelly. Even if he did not explain to Ed why he was looking for information on this Clarke fellow, he could trust Ed to be circumspect.

"I don't have to know," said Kennelly. "If you want me to help you look into this fellow, I'll do it. No questions asked."

"It's got to be absolutely off-the-record."

"Understood. Where's he from?"

"New York."

Kennelly pointed at a telephone. "Get me a line to New York. Get me through to NYPD, Homicide."

This took a little time. The White House operator said she would ring back when she established the connection. Kennelly lit a cigarette, a Lucky. Szczygiel slipped a tot of gin into a glass and tossed it back.

"I've been thinking about that note I found in Hay's apartment," said Kennelly. "It was signed 'AB for AF.' Could AB be Abbadabba Berman and AF Arthur Flegenheimer?"

"As good a guess as any," said Szczygiel.

"But still a guess," Kennelly admitted.

"I believe you said he wrote 'O.K.' on the note. That could mean that he had met the 'obligation,' whatever that was. Most simply, he paid off a loan."

"So why," asked Kennelly, "would Dutch Schultz make a loan to Ben Hay?"

Szczygiel shrugged. "They were cordial enough last night."

After eighteen minutes, the operator reported that she had the line to the New York Police Department, homicide squad, open.

"Calling for Lieutenant Tom Casey," said Kennelly. "Tell him Kennelly of D.C. Homicide is on the line."

After a little delay, Casey took the call. "Kennelly, you ol' son of a gun! What can I do for you? I bet it's sumpin', or you wouldn't call."

"Right, ol' buddy. Not a murder. I'm just trying to get a rundown on a New Yorker. Just the basic information. In confidence. Absolute confidence."

"Got it. Who you got in mind?"

"Guy by the name of Nathan Clarke. We understand he's a millionaire."

"He sure is!" said Casey. "What you want to know about him?"

"Just the usual stuff. A workup. He's not a suspect or anything like that. He might turn out to be an innocent bystander witness. Can you fill me in?"

"Give me a couple hours. I can teletype."

"Leave the guy's name off what you send. I'll know who you're talking about."

"Right. You already had the rain we're supposed to get later?"

"A lot of 'er," said Kennelly.

"We could use it. There's dust on the streets."

"Hey, Tom. There's another thing you can do for me. I'm sure you remember how Dutch Schultz was acquitted of murder two or three years ago."

"That son of a bitch beat the rap," said Casey bitterly. "But we'll get him sooner or later."

"I understand he had three alibi witnesses. Can you tell me who they were?"

"Betcha. Let's start with Antonio Flores. Tony's a fish wholesaler. Then there was Trent MacDougal. MacDougal owns a furniture store on Thirty-eighth Street. Finally, there was Leonard Nussbaum. Len has a fleet of about twenty cabs. They testified that Dutch Schultz was at a party at Polly Adler's when the murder came down. Just one witness testified he was *not* there: a lawyer by the name of Benjamin Hay."

"Did any of these guys suddenly get rich after they testified?"

"It wouldn't work that way, Kennelly. Y' gotta understand. What these guys were, was *vulnerable.* Them saying no to Dutch Schultz would not have been wise."

"Hay did."

"I figure Hay was a setup, too. In other words, Dixie Davis wanted one respectable witness to testify against Dutch. That made it look better. Of course, it was easy enough to say that Hay just happened to *miss* Dutch. All three of the others testified that Hay was with one of Polly's girls for quite a while."

"What did Polly say?" asked Kennelly.

"You wouldn't call Polly Adler for a witness, any more than you'd call Sherm Billingsley or Walter Winchell—any more than you'd call Lucky Luciano, who was there, too. Nobody would believe any one of 'em. No New Yorker would, anyway."

"I appreciate it, Tom."

"My pleasure. I'll wire you a rundown on Nathan Clarke."

5

MRS. ROOSEVELT SPENT HER afternoon reviewing correspondence, dictating letters, and returning telephone calls—until four o'clock, when she took a relaxing bath, soaking in hot, soapy water.

She left the White House not long after five, to be driven to the Abyssinian Baptist Church, where she would attend a dinner of the Washington chapter of the National Association for the Advancement of Colored People. Because the major hotels would not rent their ballrooms or serve dinners to Negroes, the NAACP met in the recreation hall of the city's largest Negro church.

The people at the church were there to address grave problems, but they did not allow that to dampen their spirits or to discourage them from having fun. They socialized exuberantly, greeting each other with friendly slaps on the back and engaging in animated, laughing conversation. Mrs. Roosevelt reflected that this innocent ebullience was part of the image of America's colored people and was a reason why so many whites could declare naively that the Negroes were discontented only to the extent that white troublemakers stirred them up, that they were in fact quite happy with their lot in life. ("They don't want to go to our movie theaters. They'd rather have their own.")

The First Lady sat down to dinner at a trestle table covered with white paper and ate fried chicken, mashed potatoes with yellow chicken gravy, and fresh buttered lima beans.

A jazz band played while the guests ate. As the dinner was nearing its end a hubbub arose at the entrance, and a distinctive man arrived, carrying a trumpet in a case.

"That's Louie Armstrong," the woman beside Mrs. Roosevelt explained.

Louis Armstrong was recognized as the world's greatest jazz trumpet stylist. He was known by the nickname Satchmo.

Armstrong and his band were playing in the ballroom of the Scott Hotel, but he had come to the church early to play a few numbers and entertain the people of the NAACP.

When he had finished, he came down from the makeshift stage. Someone handed him a glass of iced tea.

"Louie, I'd like you to meet Mrs. Roosevelt."

"I'm honored, honored," said Armstrong. "I saw you sitting over there."

"The honor is mine, Mr. Armstrong," she said.

Louis Armstrong sweated while performing, and he was wiping his forehead with a handkerchief.

"I would like to ask you two questions, if you don't mind," said the First Lady.

"Of course, Ma'am. Of course."

"Well . . . What is the origin of your nickname Satchmo? It is unique, is it not?"

He grinned. "That comes from a time when I went to England to play, a few years ago. One of the newspapers called me Satchel Mouth, 'cause I got a really big mouth. It stuck, but folks shortened it to Satchmo, and Satchmo it's been ever since."

"My second question has to do with music. You are a great master of your idiom. But do you enjoy other kinds of music, say classical music and opera?"

He grinned again, showing his big white teeth. "Oh, *yeahhh*," he said with enthusiasm, nodding. "I like *all* dat, all kinds of music. It's sooo . . . *pretty!*"

6

ED KENNELLY'S WIRE FROM New York arrived at headquarters late in the afternoon.

TO: Lieutenant Edward Kennelly, HQ DCPD Homicide.
FROM: Lieutenant Thomas Casey, HQ NYPD Homicide.
RE: Subject discussed earlier.
The subject of whom you inquired has no criminal record in this city or state. I have taken the liberty of inquiring of the FBI, which has no record of him either.

He is an exceptionally wealthy man, having inherited his fortune from his father and an uncle who owned and operated a railroad I will not name. As you suggested, he owns a yacht and cruises the world.

He has taken a number of prominent people on cruises. Among these are Al Smith this year, Vice President John Nance Garner in 1929, Thomas Alva Edison in 1928, and early this year General Douglas MacArthur. The general was accompanied by a Eurasian girl not identified.

Although the subject has no criminal record, he could have one, since he has conspicuously flouted laws that did not suit him. I need hardly mention Prohibition. In addition, he is known to carry a revolver, in violation of the Sullivan Law. What is more, he transports young women across state lines in violation of the Mann Act.

```
    Young women have complained of going
aboard his yacht for a few days' cruise, sup-
posedly to places like Maine, only to find
themselves in the Caribbean with no passports
and so the inability to go ashore.
    The subject uses his money to avoid the le-
gal consequences of his conduct.
    Advise if I can provide further informa-
tion.
```

7

RETURNING TO THE WHITE House in mid-evening, Mrs. Roosevelt found a telephone message waiting. Hick was calling from New York. The First Lady rang the operator and placed the return call.

"Well," said Hick, "your man Hay is an interesting fellow. Why he works in the White House on a White House lawyer's salary is difficult to imagine."

"It places him at the center of many things," said Mrs. Roosevelt. "It affords him many opportunities."

"Including the opportunity to assassinate the president. Is that what you have in mind?"

"Besides that, the opportunity to examine confidential documents, to overhear private conversations, and so on. The information he obtains that way might be very useful to him in choosing investments in the stock market."

"I will tell you one thing for sure," said Hick. "He does

not live on the salary of a government lawyer. When he comes to New York, he puts up in a suite in the Waldorf."

"He has a peculiar assortment of friends," said Mrs. Roosevelt.

"You have no idea *how* peculiar. To the ones you already know about, add Louis Lepke Buchalter and Albert Anastasia. Do you know who they are?

"I have heard the names," said Mrs. Roosevelt. "Gangsters. The worst, the most notorious—"

"The head men of Murder Incorporated. Hit men."

"Could they be involved in—?"

"An attempt to kill Frank? No. They are internal enforcers. They only kill their own kind, members of the Mob."

"Even so . . . for Mr. Hay to be involved with their kind is most condemnatory."

"If he's lifting confidential information, he could be giving it to them. Meyer Lansky would know how to use it."

"Have you any idea who Miss Pointer is?"

"Give me a little more time on that."

XI

1

THURSDAY MORNING WAS SUNNY and warm, and Mrs. Roosevelt took the opportunity for an early-morning ride in Rock Creek Park. Once more, her friend Elinor Morgenthau joined her.

"I've been reviewing those automobile prices we talked about last week," said Mrs. Morgenthau. "Henry still has his mind set on a Packard. Can you believe a Packard Twelve costs three thousand seven hundred and twenty dollars? At that, it's not the most expensive car on the road. I'm glad he didn't choose a Cadillac V-Sixteen, for which they ask sixty-two-fifty!"

"You can buy a nice Ford or Chevrolet for less than five hundred dollars," said the First Lady.

"If you insist on something bigger, you can buy a Hupmobile Eight for eleven ninety-five."

"I enjoyed the Auburn we once drove," said Mrs. Roosevelt.

"I've been going with Henry to look at some of these cars. Eleanor, you wouldn't believe! Some of the new cars have *no choke!*"

"Well, what do you do when the engine splutters?"

"I don't know. Somehow it fixes itself."

"The world has changed," said Mrs. Roosevelt.

They cantered along for a minute or two, in silence, enjoying the spring morning.

Then Elinor Morgenthau spoke. Apparently her mind had remained on the First Lady's comment that the world had changed. "Have you read about the scandal at the Cincinnati Zoo Opera?" she asked.

"I don't believe I have."

"Well . . . It seems that the company was doing the opera *Thaïs*. The title role was being played by the diva Leonora Corona. In the second act, the libretto calls for Thaïs to expose herself naked. This has always been done with flesh-colored tights and so on. But this prima donna threw back her cloak and exposed herself with no covering at all, except a skimpy *cache-sexe* between her hips. Cincinnati—"

"Arrested her, I should imagine," said Mrs. Roosevelt. "That city is not known for broad-mindedness."

"Actually, no," said Elinor. "The diva explained that her art required her to expose herself. If the historical Thaïs had no modesty, she could have none. It is a matter of artistic integrity."

"And the city fathers accepted that?"

"She filled the house every night for the rest of the run."

2

THE PRESIDENT DID NOT read the society news. Neither did Missy, ordinarily. But this morning she clipped a story and handed it to him at his desk—

> **GALA PARTY ON GREAT YACHT**
>
> The yacht *Neptune*, which belongs to railroad heir Nathan Clarke, is too big to navigate the Potomac as far as this city. This did not discourage Clarke from making the yacht the scene of a festive gala Tuesday night. He anchored in Chesapeake Bay, just off Annapolis, had his guests brought out in small boats, and entertained lavishly from seven until the wee hours of the morning.
>
> Among the distinguished guests on board were Italian radio scientist Guglielmo Marconi, in the company of David Sarnoff; Hollywood beauty Jean Harlow; football coach Knute Rockne; tennis champ Bill Tilden; Joseph Kennedy and his friend Gloria Swanson; and U.S. Army chief of staff General Douglas MacArthur.
>
> A few of the guests remained aboard for

> a two-or-three day cruise on the Atlantic. Among those going on the cruise were Mr. Kennedy and Miss Swanson, and General MacArthur.

The president did not return the clipping to Missy. Within a few minutes it was in a sealed envelope and on its way up to Mrs. Roosevelt in her study. She called in Stan Szczygiel and showed it to him.

Ed Kennelly was with him. She was startled when he handed the clipping to Kennelly.

"I have to confess to you, Ma'am, that I have taken Ed into our confidence—partially."

"That you know, and that I now know," she said. "No one else must know."

"Ed doesn't know why we are interested in Nathan Clarke. He just agreed to help me find out as much as he could about him. He has been very helpful."

Mrs. Roosevelt nodded. "I remain curious about the discrepancies in Miss Patchen's story. She may have had many reasons for lying to us about her egress from the Executive Wing. The night she lied about may just *happen* to be the night when Officer Douglas was killed. It may have been a coincidence, but it is a somewhat stretched coincidence, don't you agree?"

"I do. But she checked out through the west gate at seven-twenty-three. Douglas was not killed until a long time after that."

"The officer on duty at the west gate. His name is—?"

"Harrigan."

"We are placing a great deal of reliance on his word," she suggested. "We doubt Officer Slye's word that she did not pass by his desk, but we accept the word of Officer Harrigan that she did pass by his."

"And he noted her on his log," Szczygiel added.

"What sort of record has Officer Harrigan?"

"Flawless," said Szczygiel. "I checked his record. He even has a letter of commendation, signed by President Hoover."

"A married man?"

"No. A bachelor. He lives with his father and mother."

"Might he have been susceptible to Miss Patchen's conspicuous charms?"

"Suppose he was. Suppose he entered a false report on his log. She is left on the grounds, with access to the main house. But what good does that do her? Unless she knows her way around very well, she cannot reach the door to the president's bedroom."

"But someone may have led her," said Mrs. Roosevelt.

"For what reason?" Szczygiel asked.

"To catch and hold Officer Douglas's attention while her accomplice attacked and killed him."

"Isn't that a little fantastic?"

"Not necessarily," said Kennelly. "The girl is entirely willing to show herself—that is, to undress—to capture a man's attention."

"How do you know this?" asked Mrs. Roosevelt.

"Well . . . She lifted her skirt and showed me her legs. She offered to show me more if I would drop my interrogation."

"Did you find out anything?"

"Only that her father in Columbus, Ohio, is not an honest trucker but a bootlegger."

"Which leads to nothing," said the First Lady. "I am still curious about motive."

"Her father is going to lose a lot of money when Prohibition is repealed," said Kennelly. "But the death of the president would not stop that."

"I should really like to know," said Mrs. Roosevelt, "if Miss Patchen did indeed sign out at the west gate and take a cab. Perhaps you should question Harrigan again."

3

HICK CALLED FROM NEW York.

"I've got to leave for Chicago late this afternoon," she said. "I'm taking the sleeper. In the meantime, though, I've come up with some information on Jo Pointer."

"I should be happy to have it."

"I think it's interesting, Pussy—I guess I shouldn't call you that on the telephone."

"Perhaps not."

"Anyway . . . Miss Jo Pointer is more than a little notorious in New York. She's got money. She's got a lot of money. She spends a lot of money. She has no apparent source of it, so it must be family money. I don't know the name Pointer. Neither does anyone else."

"Pointer . . ." said Mrs. Roosevelt. "I don't think I've ever heard the name before."

"She's in and out of town a lot and lives in hotels when she's here. She has been seen in the company of some of Mr. Hay's friends, like Bugsy Siegel. The word is around that she has fallen in love with Ben Hay and has moved to Washington to be with him. The word is also around that she is not going to tolerate Washington for long—she calls it a hick town—and will demand that Hay leave government service and come back here with her. Obviously he does not need his salary."

"Does he have a family?"

"His father is a lawyer, retired now. His mother is a commercial artist who does illustrations for advertisements. They are prosperous people, but they don't put up in suites in the Waldorf."

"We must discover the source of his income," said Mrs. Roosevelt. "I am afraid it comes from his friends in the Mob."

4

AT ED KENNELLY'S REQUEST, Stan Szczygiel telephoned the headquarters of the Coast Guard. Hearing that the call was from a Secret Service agent, a commander took it.

"I have a very simple question," Szczygiel told him. "A yacht called *Neptune*, owned by a Mr. Nathan Clarke, sailed from Annapolis on Wednesday morning, supposedly to go down Chesapeake Bay and out into the Atlantic for a cruise up or down the coast. I would like to know if that yacht is still at sea, if it has called at any port, and if it has been met by any other boat to which passengers might have been transferred."

"That will take a little while to find out," said the commander.

"Please do and call me back."

5

WHILE WAITING TO HEAR from the Coast Guard, Szczygiel called Officer Lemuel Harrigan to his office.

Harrigan was a thirty-year-old, a man of no great presence, a bland face with no memorable features. He spoke with a distinctive accent, though—a unique combination of an Irish brogue and the Southern drawl of many Washingtonians.

"Do Ah knoo her? Uv *course*. Not a man works in the Whaat House that doesn't know Angie. She's a flairt."

"A flirt," said Szczygiel. "Has she ever gone beyond flirting with you?"

"Nay, Sor. Nay. Fer sure."

"Does she go beyond flirting with others?"

"I would not know, Sor."

"Have you heard rumors that she does?"

"Nay, Sor."

"Well, what about Bob Hogan?"

"Ah wouldn' know. Ah hearn no rumors about that."

"But you are absolutely certain that Angela Patchen checked out at your desk at seven-twenty-three Friday night."

"She did that, Sor. Uhh . . . May Ah ask whaa about it is so important?"

"I'm sure you know that Officer Douglas was murdered in the White House that night. Angela checked out of the grounds at your station, but she did not check out of the West Wing."

"McKay—"

"McKay wasn't on duty Friday night. He was scheduled for it, but he had an emergency appendectomy that afternoon, and Frank Slye took his place."

"Slye . . . !"

"And Slye insists she never came past his desk."

"Well . . . She came baa maan. Ah couldn't be wrong. She . . . she's a girl you gonna *remember.*"

"Just keep it in mind that a murder was committed in the White House that night," said Szczygiel firmly. "It is not just a matter of somebody trespassing. It's a matter of *murder.*"

Harrigan looked stricken. Szczygiel decided he was lying.

6

THE COAST GUARD COMMANDER called back.

"The yacht *Neptune* rounded Cape Charles about ten A.M. Wednesday and proceeded out into the Atlantic. It passed off Atlantic City and may be on its way to New York. It has entered no port. So far as a rendezvous with another yacht or boat, we have no sighting that indicates it. We can't, of course, say for certain that it didn't happen. It may, for example, have met with a bootlegger boat and taken on a load of liquor. That would have been at night, most likely."

"I appreciate the information," said Szczygiel.

"Do you want us to put the yacht under special surveillance?" the commander asked. "We have a dirigible working off the New Jersey coast and could keep watch."

"You've done everything that's necessary, Commander. And thanks again."

Szczygiel picked up the telephone to convey this word to Kennelly.

7

THE HOTEL CHASTLETON WAS not one of the city's most luxurious. Neither was it modest. It was a medium-high-price hotel where visiting businessmen sometimes stayed. It had a reputation out of town for affording guests female companionship, if they wished—which was nothing special; hardly a hotel in Washington didn't.

Ed Kennelly arrived late in the afternoon and showed his shield to the desk clerk before asking the room number of Miss Cooper.

"I'm not supposed to—"

"You want to get your ass in deep trouble, don't give me the number," Kennelly growled. He was an old-fashioned Irish cop, and he steamed at resistance. "What's it gonna be, sonny?"

The clerk blanched and gave him the number.

"Is she alone?"

"So far as I know, Sir."

"Her friend is not in the hotel?"

"Uhh . . . No, Sir."

"If he comes in, ring the room before he can get up there. We know who I'm talking about. Also, the fact that I'm here is police business and not to be mentioned to anyone. Got that?"

"Yes, Sir."

He pushed the button to ring the bell in the suite General MacArthur rented for Isabel Cooper. She opened the door.

She was as she had been described: consummately beautiful, possessed by an ethereal beauty that defined her. She was Eurasian, the daughter of a Chinese mother and a Scottish father. Her eyes were dark and solemn. Her nose was delicate and slightly flat for Western tastes. Her complexion was white and satin-smooth. Her hair was glossy black. He guessed she was less than twenty years old.

She was wearing a silk dress of emerald green, embroidered with gold and silver thread. The collar was high. Though the skirt was ankle length, it was slit two thirds of the way up her thighs, revealing shapely bare legs. The silk clung to her and suggested the outlines of her figure. Kennelly did not know this, but the dress was what the Chinese called a cheongsam.

"Miss Cooper?"

"Yes."

"I am Lieutenant Edward Kennelly of the homicide squad, D.C. police. I'd like to talk to you for a few minutes. May I come in?"

She stepped away from the door and with her arm beckoned him to enter.

The small living room of her suite was furnished in a style that had gone out with the World War. The Victorian settee was graceful, though a little too heavy, and upholstered in black horsehair. Two chairs, one a rocker, were in the same style. The room had long been lighted by oil lamps, and these had been converted to burn electric bulbs. The walls were covered with red brocade, rather dark and gloomy to Kennelly's taste. The only modern thing in the room was a radio set, an old one with speaker set in a horn.

"Policeman," Isabel said apprehensively. "Is trouble?"

"No. Not at all. I only want to ask you a few questions. There is no trouble."

"You like tea?" she asked.

"Well . . . I don't want to put you to—"

"Is pleasure," she said. "Water is already hot."

She left the room. He looked around. He saw no sign of the general, nothing that might have been personal to him. No boots. No cap. No photos. It seemed to him that Isabel Cooper was living an isolated life in this little suite.

She returned, carrying a tray on which sat a teapot and two little cups without handles. She poured. They sipped.

"You like this?" she asked.

"Uh . . . Well, yes. It's—"

"Is ginseng," she said. "Very good for you. Good for many . . . sick." She smiled shyly. "Also, they say, make . . . sexy." She shrugged. "No need."

"No. Uh. I want to ask you about the general. It would be well if you don't tell him I asked."

She frowned. " 'Homicide,' " she said. "This means . . . murder. Dougy." She pronounced it "Duggy." "He no—"

"No, not at all," Kennelly assured her. "I just want to ask about a friend of his."

"Yes? I no know his friends. He not want Pinky to know about me." Pinky was the nickname of MacArthur's mother. "No?"

Kennelly sipped the ginseng tea. It could become an

acquired taste, he decided. She poured more into his tiny cup.

"Where is the general now?" he asked.

"On yacht," she said. "With girl probably. Sometimes *I* go on yacht. Not now."

"And this yacht belongs to Mr. Nathan Clarke."

"Nat. Yes. Belong Nat. Big boat. Big for here. In Shanghai, Hong Kong—" She flared her nostrils scornfully. "Nat big rich man . . . for American."

"The general brought you here from—?"

"Manila. I go there with other man. Dougy, he see. He want. I agree. Dougy is *beautiful* man!"

"So he brought you to Washington."

"Is sadness. I no like here. Live here, in these rooms. Never go nowhere. I make him buy me car and hire me chauffeur, so I can go around Washington. But chauffeur cannot drive me home."

"So you have a suite in this hotel, a car, and a chauffeur. That must cost the general a lot of money."

"Rich friends," she said simply.

"Like Nathan Clarke?"

"Oh, Nat, he lend Dougy many money."

"Others?" Kennelly asked.

"I no know, really. But Nat lend Dougy. I think Nat pay rent on these rooms. I think Nat buy car, pay chauffeur. So Pinky not find out." She shrugged. "Anyway, Dougy no have so much money. Not rich man. All time army officer. His father army officer. Where come so much money?"

"So you want to go home?" Kennelly asked sympathetically.

She shook her head sadly. "Never go. Many far. Besides, now war. Soon bigger war. No home no more."

8

EARLY IN THE EVENING, Mrs. Roosevelt placed a telephone call to New York, to Congressman Fiorello LaGuardia.

"How nice of you to take my call, Mr. LaGuardia."

"How nice of you to call. Of course, one could hardly refuse to accept a telephone call from a First Lady—not even Florence Kling Harding."

"Oh, Mr. LaGuardia, don't compare me to that woman."

"Not at all. It is very pleasant to hear from you. I haven't seen you since—"

"Since the inaugural ball," she said.

"Well . . . If I become mayor of the city, as I intend to do, I will be spending all my time in New York."

"You have my very best wishes," she said. "Unofficially."

LaGuardia laughed that rasping little laugh that was characteristic of him. "I'd treasure your endorsement above all others," he said.

"I'm not sure it would do you any good. I seem to have become highly controversial."

"If I were you, Eleanor, I'd take the attacks on you as among the highest honors you could receive—considering the source. Anyway, is there anything I can do for you?"

"Perhaps," she said. "You seem to know everyone in New York. I thought I did, but I seem to have circulated within limited perimeters."

"You know all the best people."

"You know *all* the people, best and otherwise. Which is why I wanted to ask if you have ever heard the name Jo Pointer. Uh . . . a woman. Not Joseph Pointer, but Jo, perhaps Josephine."

"What do you want to know about her?"

"Who is she?"

"She's from somewhere in the Midwest, I think maybe Detroit. She is, from what I gather, the daughter of a very wealthy family, probably not named Pointer. She's a black sheep some way, possibly illegitimate. Do you know what a remittance man was?"

"The son of a prominent European family, sent to this country, and sent a generous allowance on condition he never return home."

"Exactly. I suspect Jo Pointer is a remittance woman."

XII

1

MAGGIE SAT IN THE middle of the president's bed, her head tipped as she made little sounds to remind him that he should hand her another bite of toast or bacon. She wagged her tail. The president could not resist her and reached to put a scrap of bacon into her mouth. Maggie, of course, swallowed it whole. She was all dog, but somehow he could imagine that the bite of bacon had made her smile.

Mrs. Roosevelt sat to one side of the bed and watched tolerantly. She loved the dog—but not enough to let it sit on her bed and to feed bits of her breakfast to it.

"Your circle of acquaintance is far broader than mine, Franklin," she said. "I've come across a name and wonder if it means anything to you."

The president pushed aside some of the newspapers that surrounded him on his bed. He picked up his holder and drew smoke from his Camel. "Something to do with your Hawkshawing?" he asked.

"In fact, yes. Have you ever head of a very wealthy family named Pointer, perhaps in the Midwest?"

"Pointer. No. In what context does this come up?"

"We have to remain suspicious of Mr. Ben Hay. He has some evil friends, members of the New York Mob. He lives in an apartment here in Washington, in circumstances his income would not allow. Living with him is a young woman called Miss Jo Pointer. We cannot seem to find out who she is, except that she is known in New York for having and spending a very great deal of money. Congressman LaGuardia suspects she is some wealthy family's black sheep—an illegitimate daughter maybe—who is supplied with funds to secure her silence. It's not an unheard of arrangement, you know."

"Pointer . . . No, I know no family by that name."

"Alright. I thought I would ask."

"Sorry."

"Thank you anyway. Incidentally, Mr. Nathan Clarke is cruising aboard his luxurious yacht, off the New Jersey coast. He has guests on board: Mr. Joseph Kennedy, Miss Gloria Swanson, and General Douglas MacArthur."

"Odd collection," said the president.

"Very odd."

She got up and moved toward the door.

"Oh, Babs. Wait a minute. Pointer . . . A very wealthy Midwestern family. Uh . . . This is almost certainly meaningless, but the Edsel Ford family keeps homes at Grosse Pointe. Suppose this young woman is forbidden to use the name Ford. So she calls herself by the name of the family compound: Pointe, Pointer."

"We know very well who the members of the Ford family are," said the First Lady.

"Do we? Could it be that this young woman is paid a generous allowance to stay away from Grosse Pointe and not use the name Ford?" He shrugged. "A thought."

"An illegitimate daughter?" asked Mrs. Roosevelt. "Of . . . of whom?"

"Edsel," said the president.

"No. Mr. Edsel Ford is only thirty-five years old. Miss Pointer is in her mid-twenties, as I should judge."

"Henry? I hardly think so. The old devil has never been up to that sort of thing, that I've heard of."

"Now that I think of it," said Mrs. Roosevelt, "she said she occasionally flies to Detroit. When she said she flew in a Ford Tri-Motor, Mr. Hay grinned and said, 'What else?' "

"Mr. Ford, Mr. *Henry* Ford, would have been in his vigorous forties when Miss Pointer was born," said the president.

"This is inconceivable," said the First Lady.

The president shrugged. "Is it important?"

"Maybe not."

2

"I'VE LOST MY PATIENCE with the evasions and maybe outright lies of some of our uniformed officers," complained Stan Szczygiel. "Either Angela Patchen stayed all night, or she didn't. I suggest we call in Harrigan and Slye and get this straightened out once and for all."

Mrs. Roosevelt nodded. So did Ed Kennelly, more vigorously.

Within a few minutes, the two officers sat uneasily in the First Lady's study, facing a stern Szczygiel and a grim Kennelly.

"Alright," said Szczygiel. "One of you is lying. Either Angela Patchen went by your station on Friday night, on her way out of the West Wing and on her way off the White House grounds, or she didn't. So, which was it? Did she or didn't she?"

Frank Slye was adamant. "She did *not* pass my desk! Why would I say she did?"

Harrigan said nothing.

Mrs. Roosevelt prompted him. "Mr. Harrigan?"

"I suppose I lose my job," he said disconsolately. "She did not go out through the west gate. I falsified the log."

"*Why?*" Szczygiel demanded.

Harrigan drew a deep breath. "Bob Hogan paid me to do it," he said hoarsely. "He gave me fifty dollars."

"Why?"

"He and Angela spent the night together, somewhere in the White House. He paid McKay, too. If McKay had been on duty—that is, hadn't gone in to have his appendix taken out—it would have worked. No one would have been the wiser."

"They didn't spend the night in the White House," said Slye. "They couldn't have got out of the West Wing."

Mrs. Roosevelt raised her eyebrows high. "Miss Patchen did somehow manage to leave the grounds," she said. "She signed in at the northwest gate on Saturday morning."

"The west gate is locked at midnight," said Harrigan. "No one is on duty there after midnight. But there's a key in the office. Hogan could have taken the key and let her out."

"Have we checked the logs for Mr. Hogan?" asked the First Lady. "Is there record for *his* having left and returned?"

"No," said Szczygiel. "I didn't think it likely . . . I didn't think it *possible* that one of the uniformed officers could have—"

"Am I fired?" Harrigan asked.

"Not for the moment," said Szczygiel. "It depends on two things—first, on what we find out that Hogan and Angela really did that night; and, second, that you keep this entire matter confidential."

"I promise you something," said Harrigan, almost tearful. "I took his fifty dollars to fudge the log so he could have his night with Angie, since that was what he wanted; but I would not, for *any* amount of money, have let a stranger *come in*. I guess I'm stupid, but—"

"You're stupid," Szczygiel agreed.

When the two officers were gone, Szczygiel frowned hard and said, "If we fire him, he might blab. He may think of that. I'm afraid we're between the devil and the deep blue sea on this."

3

"I SHOULD LIKE TO know if the FBI has any information in its files on Miss Pointer," said the First Lady.

"I can arrange to have an inquiry made from D.C. headquarters," said Kennelly. "No one has to know the inquiry comes from here."

"Would you do that, please?"

"It would be better if we had a set of her fingerprints."

"I'm afraid we haven't any. I can hardly invite her to the White House for tea."

"I can get them," said Kennelly.

He put a man on the street outside Hay's apartment. He made a telephone call to the apartment, and a woman answered. An hour later, her V-12 Lincoln arrived, and the woman came out and got in it. The man on the street called Kennelly, who arrived in minutes. He went to the door of the apartment and rang the bell. When no one responded, he let himself in.

He was in the apartment less than two minutes. He knew what he wanted. He went straight to the bathroom and picked up a tortoiseshell compact, initialed *JP*. It was the sort of personal item only the woman would have used; also the kind of item she would suppose she had misplaced and would dream had been stolen.

At headquarters, technicians lifted the fingerprints, and a junior detective delivered them to the FBI fingerprint lab.

4

"IT WOULD APPEAR," SAID Mrs. Roosevelt to Angela Patchen, "that you have not told us the truth. Unless you do so now, you will be arrested by marshals and conveyed to the federal prison in the navy yard."

"No!"

"Miss Patchen, you did not check out of the West Wing last Friday night. You did not leave the grounds through the west gate at seven-twenty-three," said Szczygiel. "Bob Hogan bribed Harrigan to say you left at that time, and to falsify the log. I suppose he bribed McKay also, but McKay was in the hospital when the time came for him to write your name in his log. So . . . What do you have to tell us?"

The young woman began to cry. "It was s'pposed to work," she sobbed. "I came out the door, and there was Slye where McKay was s'pposed to be. I went straight to Bob and told him. He said not to worry, that everything would work out okay."

"What was your purpose in all of this?" asked Mrs. Roosevelt.

Angela rubbed the tears from her cheeks. "All we wanted to do was—" She sobbed. "All we wanted to do was . . . what bad girls do."

"Where were you going to do this?" asked Szczygiel.

"In one of the bedrooms on the third floor."

"And where *did* you do it?" asked Szczygiel. "I assume you did."

"We did it in the vice president's office. We knew Mr. Garner would not be coming by in the evening."

"No one checked that office all night?"

"We latched the door. We did not turn on the lights. I stood at the window and stared out at the lights of the city, coming down mostly off the clouds." She sniffled. "You remember it rained hard that night. I was quite naked, but I knew no one could see me; no one would be out there on the lawn in that rain. We did . . . what we did on Mr. Garner's big leather couch. The room smells of his cigars. Bob found a bottle of bourbon in his desk. We drank some of it, straight. Bob said Mr. Garner would never remember how much was left in that quart."

"How long did you remain in Mr. Garner's office?" asked Mrs. Roosevelt.

"All night, almost. It was a glorious night."

"Then you got out of the West Wing and off the grounds," said Szczygiel. "How did you work that?"

"Bob had keys. After the rain stopped, we went out the window. Bob unlocked the west gate and let me out."

"Are you in love with Officer Hogan?" asked Mrs. Roosevelt.

"Bob is married. He has kids. It would be silly to love him. But I'd like to spend another night with him. Somewhere else."

5

"MA'AM," SAID TOMMY. "LISTEN!"

Mrs. Roosevelt put down her pen and lifted her chin.

The drone of engines was unmistakable. She had heard that distinctive sound twice before.

"Well," she said. "We'd best go out and look."

They went downstairs and walked out on the South Portico. They stared up. The drone grew louder. They stared at the sky and shortly saw a huge silver dirigible floating majestically above the city. It was unbelievably big, and, unlike an airplane, it had no need to maintain speed to keep it aloft. It drifted across the sky, slowly, gracefully, with imperturbable dignity, moved by four engines that were not laboring.

This rigid airship belonged to the U.S. Navy; and, though one had crashed in a storm last month, few believed otherwise than that helium-buoyed dirigibles represented the future of air transportation. There was talk of vacations in Europe, of crossing the Atlantic in less than half the time of the fastest liner. The cabins of a dirigible, though not nearly as spacious, could be as luxurious, almost, as those aboard the *Queen Mary*. German zeppelins, floating with hydrogen, carried passengers all around Germany and the rest of Europe. The finest food was served to the passengers, who looked down on the earth as they passed above it at a leisurely pace. Some of the zeppelins had piano lounges. All had bars. Most offered sleeping accommodations.

Flying in an airplane was an adventure, risked only by the hurried and bold. Despite efforts to make them so, passengers could not be comfortable as the plane hurtled through the air, maneuvering, bouncing on what they called air pockets, and noisy with the roar of straining engines. The airship was sedate, quiet, and reassuring as it glided smoothly across the sky.

Work had come to a standstill in all of Washington. Many offices were vacant. People had come out on the streets to stare at the sky. The president himself had been wheeled from his office so he could look at the airship.

As decorously as it had appeared, the dirigible disappeared, the drone of its engines fading as it passed over the horizon and out of sight.

Mrs. Roosevelt returned to her study.

6

LATER IN THE AFTERNOON Ed Kennelly brought her the report from the FBI fingerprint lab—

CONFIDENTIAL FROM THE

FEDERAL BUREAU OF INVESTIGATION

TO: Lieutenant Edward Kennelly, District of Columbia Police Department, Homicide Division.

FROM: Glenn Ahern, Agent and Laboratory Administrator, Federal Bureau of Investigation.

IN RE: Fingerprints submitted.

We have run the submitted prints through our files. They are the fingerprints of one Betty Nans, whose last known address was 1117 West Chicago Avenue, Detroit, Michigan.

The subject was arrested on July 24, 1928, on a charge of violating the Volstead Act by possessing and selling intoxicating liquors. She was released on July 26, on a $5,000 bond, and the matter was subsequently dropped.

Information adduced during her brief confinement was added to the file. The subject was reared in a private boarding school for girls in Lorain County, Ohio. She ran away on a number of occasions and was subsequently moved to a more restrictive school in Detroit. She was a ward of the Juvenile Court.

Subsequent to her arrest in 1928 this bureau has no further record of her.

"Changed her name," Kennelly said to Mrs. Roosevelt and Szczygiel when he showed them the FBI report.

"It seems extremely unlikely that the elegant Miss Pointer and the girl who was a ward of the juvenile court and later arrested for selling liquor are the same person," said the First Lady.

"Detroit," said Kennelly. "The Purple Gang. If she was selling liquor in Detroit, she had to be doing it with the approval of thc Purple Gang. Also, that explains her connection with the New York Mob. The Purple Gang has been broken up, but she could have moved on, with top-notch credentials."

"I suppose it also explains where she got the bail money and who caused the matter to be dropped," said Szczygiel.

"All very well," said Mrs. Roosevelt, "but what does any of this have to do with what we suspect of Mr. Hay?"

"Maybe nothing," said Kennelly. "But an effective investigative technique is to accumulate every scrap of information you can about a suspect."

"Including the exculpatory?" she asked.

"Including the exculpatory."

"Very well. We know Mr. Hay was in the White House all night. We know he had served here long enough to understand the security system. We know he had been seen here so long that officers might see nothing suspicious in his being on the second floor in mid-evening. We know he was an expert with the weapon used: the bayonet."

"Yes. Yes," said Szczygiel. "What we don't know is—"

"That he in fact meant to do harm to the president. And if he did, *why?* What was his motive?"

"I wonder if he could be a contract killer," said Kennelly. "Let me get Tom Casey on the phone again."

While they waited for the call to go through, they talked about Angela Patchen and Bob Hogan.

"We have the same problem," said Mrs. Roosevelt. "I cannot imagine what motive could have moved them."

"Hogan gave Harrigan fifty dollars and was prepared to give McKay another fifty," said Kennelly. "That's a hundred dollars to buy a night with Angie Patchen. She wouldn't have charged him anything, and he could have rented a hotel room for two dollars. All he had to do was meet her when she got off work. Why the trouble, risk, and expense?"

"You're suggesting?"

"Why was it worth a hundred dollars to him to keep Angie in the White House after she'd supposedly checked out? My guess is money. Somebody was going to pay Hogan and Angie a lot more than a hundred dollars for assistance with something. Or for doing it."

"How?" asked Szczygiel.

"Okay," said Kennelly. "Angie is east in the hall, smiling big at Doug Douglas and raising her skirt or unbuttoning her blouse. Douglas is glassy eyed, all his attention on her. Hogan comes out of a room across the hall and stabs him. Or somebody else does. How about somebody with known training and experience with the bayonet?"

A minute or so later the telephone rang. The call to the New York Police Department, to Lieutenant Tom Casey, had been completed.

Mrs. Roosevelt and Stan Szczygiel could only hear the Kennelly side of the conversation—

*** "Right! Right. Listen, I do appreciate the information you sent me. Knew I could count on you, Tom. You call on me when you need to." *** "Glad to hear it. Laid the dust, huh? Boy, they could use it a lot of other places." *** " 'Kay. Hey, Tom, I need to ask you somethin'. Don't go researching on it. Just tell me if you know. Have you got a stone killer working New York occasionally who uses a bayonet? Or a big, heavy knife? I'm lookin' at a maybe hit man who uses a bayonet." *** "Uh-huh. Uh-huh. Right. Well . . . Hey, thanks. I appreciate it. Gimme a call anytime."

He put down the telephone. "There's a whole lot of murders in New York. Guns, mostly. And knives, yes; and big knives that might be bayonets, yes. But the knife killings are not contract killings, so far as he can tell. They're guys on a rampage. Italians cut each other. Negroes cut each other. The hoi polloi would rather shoot each other. He's got one or two unsolved knife murders, but the circumstances don't suggest a paid hit."

7

THE TELEPHONE RANG AGAIN that evening in the president's bedroom. Missy knew it was going to be another unwanted call.

The candlestick telephone was equipped with an auxiliary earpiece. Missy handed it to the president so he could hear the conversation.

"Missy? Nat."

"You again! What do I have to do to make you stop doing this?"

"Give it up. Come away with me."

"Away with you . . . I wouldn't walk across the street with you."

"I'm calling you ship to shore, by radio, from my boat. We're off Atlantic City, on our way back to Annapolis."

Missy pulled on her peignoir, which had fallen open, revealing more of her silk nightgown than she felt comfortable showing.

"We can be married at Annapolis."

"We *could* maybe, but we're not going to be. Can't you get that through your mind? What do I have to say? What do I have to do to make you understand?"

"Look, Missy . . . I love you. I want you. I can make you happier than you've ever been."

"I wouldn't be."

The president smoked the Camel in his holder, listening grimly to the conversation.

"Think of this, darling. It's not too late for us to have kids. Wouldn't that be glorious?"

"No, it wouldn't be glorious."

"You are never going to have kids with that crippled old man. I guess you think you love him, but it can't be."

Tears filled Missy's eyes as she saw Effdee wince.

"Nathan, if you don't leave me alone I'm going to have to have the law on you."

"People have tried that before. But you're going to see how right I am. I bought you a wonderful nightgown. It's in the master bedroom on my yacht. I want to see you in it."

"You never will," she sobbed as she hung up.

XIII

1

"ENOUGH!" THE PRESIDENT SNAPPED at Mrs. Roosevelt. "This is, by God, enough. Something has got to be done about this fellow. He's making Missy unhappy. She deserves protection."

They sat in the Oval Office. The president leaned forward over his desk as if to speak more closely with the First Lady.

"Do you want to hear what he said about me? He said I was a crippled old man who could not make a woman happy."

"That is intolerably cruel, Franklin."

"Ah! I've had worse said about me. But I should like to be able to protect my women. Including you. The things said about you are worse than what is said about me."

"Such as that I had sex with a Negro sharecropper,"

she said calmly. "I've heard it many times. It is mentioned in letters I receive."

"The difference between you and Missy is that you can protect yourself. You are the First Lady of the land. Besides, you are a strong personality. Missy is helpless in the face of something like this."

"I know a police officer," she said, "who would be glad to waylay the man and beat him senseless. Of course—"

"Of course we can do no such thing, no matter what the provocation."

"Burden of office," she said.

"What do we know about the man that we could maybe use against him."

"He seems to have made large loans—large gifts, in fact—to General MacArthur."

"Why would he do that?"

She shrugged. "I can't imagine that the general sells government contracts. That's not like him."

"I'd look for something else," said the president.

2

THE COAST GUARD REPORTED to Stan Szczygiel that the *Neptune* had anchored off Annapolis about nine in the morning. Ed Kennelly put detectives to work checking with the major hotels. Nathan Clarke had checked in at the Mayflower late in the morning. Joseph Kennedy, too—and Gloria Swanson, in a separate suite.

Mrs. Roosevelt called Kennedy.

"I should like a few minutes' conversation with you, Joe," she told him.

"Could you join me for lunch?" he asked. "We can have it in my suite."

Joseph Kennedy had contributed heavily to FDR's 1932 campaign and was a personal friend of the Roosevelts. He was a Boston banker. Lately he had invested substantially in Hollywood film production.

He greeted the First Lady cordially at the door to his posh suite.

"Come in, Eleanor, do come in! I don't believe you've met Gloria Swanson."

She hadn't met her but had seen the famous actress in several films. For a few years Gloria Swanson had been the most popular actress in Hollywood, in silent films chiefly, lately in sound. It was said of her now that she had passed the peak of her career, though she was only thirty-six years old. Kennedy was financing for her a venture into film production. The further word was that she and Joseph Kennedy were engaged in a torrid liaison that had gone on for some months.

Gloria Swanson was smaller than the First Lady had supposed: smaller and more delicate. She was easily recognizable, though, for her wide slash of a mouth and wide-open eyes. She was wearing a dress that was not for lunchtime and emphatically out of style besides: a shimmering sequin-studded silk that flowed over her like water.

Kennedy and Swanson were sharing a bottle of champagne, and he took the bottle from the ice bucket and poured a flute of it for Mrs. Roosevelt without asking if she wanted it.

"You've never paid much attention to Prohibition, have you, Joe?"

"Neither has Frank," said Kennedy.

"Prohibition is for the Bible-Belt boobs," said Gloria Swanson scornfully.

Mrs. Roosevelt sipped the champagne. She knew enough about champagne to know that this was of the very finest quality—doubtless from France and probably imported by Joe Kennedy himself, or so the rumor went.

"I need to speak in confidence," she said.

"We can slip into a bedroom," said Kennedy. "Gloria won't be offended."

"Perhaps that won't be necessary," said Mrs. Roosevelt. "I am willing to take Miss Swanson's word that she will keep this confidence."

"As you wish," said Gloria Swanson. "*I* can go in the bedroom. You do have my word that I won't betray your confidence."

The First Lady nodded. "That will be satisfactory," she said. "I am not going to reveal much, in any case."

"Go ahead, Eleanor."

"Alright. You just spent a few days in the company of Mr. Nathan Clarke. Mr. Clarke, unhappily, has been making a nuisance of himself, in a manner I won't describe. He seems to be a friend of yours, Joe. Is there anything you can tell me about him?"

"Nat?" Kennedy said with a casual shrug. "Nat is a lovable egomaniac. He's got money he hasn't even counted. Inherited. When he was a boy, his father wouldn't give him any responsibility or let him do anything useful. He's having revenge on his father by spending every damned cent the old man slaved to accumulate."

"Nat is a *nut*," said Gloria Swanson. "A . . . *nut*. Don't ask me to go on another boat ride with him."

"He was in a mood," said Kennedy. "He spent a lot of time in his cabin—sulking, I guess."

"Thank God for Dougy," said Gloria Swanson. She, too, pronounced it "Duggy." "He knew how to stroke the guy."

"They are good friends?" asked Mrs. Roosevelt. "I mean General MacArthur and Mr. Clarke."

"The best," said Kennedy. "I could be all wrong, but I have a feeling that Nat has lent Doug some money, maybe a whole lot of money. Doug would need it, you know. He's living well beyond his means."

"Nat's a *nut*," Gloria Swanson repeated.

3

ENTERING HAY'S APARTMENT WITHOUT a warrant was illegal, Kennelly knew; but he had a sense he might still find something there; and on Friday afternoon he did what he had done before: first he waited until Jo Pointer left in her Lincoln V-12, and then he entered the premises without authority.

This time he was more interested in the woman than in the man.

Her clothes, hanging in the bedroom closet and folded in the bureau drawers, were conspicuously expensive. She wore nothing cheap. He examined the labels in some of her dresses. Two of them read—

LA FARGE

Modister

DETROIT

Pontchartrain

CADILLAC SQUARE

He went through some other things. A pearl necklace lay in a leather presentation case. The label in gilt on the silk inside cover read—

LOCKHART

DEARBORN

A key he found in a drawer was for a deposit box at Chase Bank, New York.

Then he found a bank book. It, too, was from Chase Bank. The account was in the name Betty Nans. When last updated, two weeks ago, the account held $28,426.14. On that date, Betty Nans had deposited $4,000. She had deposited that amount a month before, the month before that, and so on. The bank book did not disclose the origin of the deposits; but it seemed unlikely any stock paid an equal dividend monthly, or even that bonds paid the same exact amount each month.

Kennelly would have liked to know where the money came from but knew he could not find out; the bank would never disclose, absent a court order he could hardly get.

She had a checkbook as well, on Farmers and Mechanics National Bank: a Washington bank. This account was in the name Jo Pointer. She deposited to that account irregularly, but the deposits to the checking account matched withdrawals from the Chase Bank.

Each month she wrote a check to Benjamin Hay in the amount of one hundred dollars. Ed Kennelly guessed that might be her share of the rent on the apartment.

Exploring further, he found nothing in the rooms that suggested the name Betty Nans. He remembered that the compact he had taken for fingerprints had borne the initials *JP*.

A silver cigarette case carried an engraved inscription: *JP from NC*.

Why did she want two names? Why did nothing bear the initials *BN?*

Since he had seen her leave just before he entered, he judged he had time to complete his exploration of the cubbyholes in Hay's desk, which on Tuesday he thought he lacked time to explore fully.

He found no checkbook. Hay had a checking account, and likely he carried the checkbook with him, so Kennelly could not see what checks he wrote. His passbook indicated deposits of $250 a month: his salary. He also made irregular deposits in substantial amounts and kept a balance substantially greater than might be expected of a man with that salary. Nothing suggested the origin of those deposits.

He had, though, withdrawn $1,000 in cash on April 21. Kennelly recalled the note signed "AB for AF" and reminding Hay of an obligation. Hay had noted "Okay" on April 24. Was it possible that he had withdrawn that $1,000 and carried the cash to New York over the weekend to pay AF?

And could it be possible that AF was Arthur Flegenheimer—Dutch Schultz?

If so, Mrs. Roosevelt would ask the pregnant question: Then tell me, what has any of this got to do with an apparent attempt on the life of the president?

4

"NANS . . ." SAID THE FIRST Lady. "Nans. This may be a long way from anything that amounts to anything, but it is customary in some parts of the country to name an illegitimate child in the form of a possessive of the mother's first name. I met a man once whose name was Bill Janes. He was the illegitimate child of a young woman named Jane. So . . . it is possible—I say *possible* and not more—that Miss Pointer is the illegitimate daughter of a woman named Nan."

"Whose father feels obliged to pay her four thousand dollars a month?" asked Szczygiel.

"She changes her name," said Mrs. Roosevelt, "because wherever she goes, in the Midwest anyway, she is identified as—"

"A bastard," said Kennelly.

"It must be like wearing Hester Prynne's *A*," said Mrs. Roosevelt. "A mark of shame."

"To send her that much of an allowance, the man must be immensely wealthy," said Szczygiel. "Unless she was maybe a witness to some serious crime committed by the Purple Gang and these payments are her hush money."

Kennelly shook his head emphatically. "No. If guys of that kind wanted to keep her quiet, they'd keep her quiet—and not by paying her money."

Mrs. Roosevelt asked the question Kennelly had anticipated. "Alright. What does any of this have to do with a supposed assault on the president?"

Kennelly had rehearsed his answer. "We have to take an interest in the connection between Ben Hay and Miss Pointer, on the one hand, and people like Dutch Schultz and Bugsy Siegel, on the other. Not to mention the chiefs of Murder Incorporated: Louis Lepke Buchalter and Albert Anastasia."

"I still must ask, why would any one of these gentlemen want to assassinate the president?"

"It's not like them, I must say," Kennelly admitted. "Murder Incorporated is an enforcement agency for the Mob. They kill their own."

"Well, I have a question," said Mrs. Roosevelt.

She had seen to it that the two men had sips of their favorite potables, together with tiny sandwiches of lunch meat and cheese. She herself nibbled on a bit of cheese and sipped lemonade.

"Which question is?"

"We have assumed from the very beginning that Officer Douglas Douglas was an innocent victim. Is there any possibility that the person who murdered him came to murder *him*, not the president?"

"I've gone all through his personnel file," said Szczygiel. "It is flawless."

"An irregularity of the kind that would inspire his murder would probably not appear in his file," said the First Lady. "Did he live better than his wage would have allowed, for example?"

"I think not," said Szczygiel. "His home seems ordinary, appropriate to a man holding his job."

"It's an unusual man who doesn't have *something* to hide," Kennelly observed.

"Let us not distress poor Mrs. Douglas," said Mrs. Roosevelt, "but let us see if we can discover any irregularities about Officer Douglas."

5

ED KENNELLY WORKED WITH Stan Szczygiel, and it took him very little time to find anomalies in the record of Officer Douglas Douglas. The Secret Service agent had to rely on the files. The homicide detective did not.

Kennelly was also in a position to exert pressure on certain people. He checked with bookies.

The first four visits were not productive. The fifth was.

"Ed, for God's sake! You never asked me to—"

"I never involved you in a murder investigation before."

The bookie was a Negro, as were most, not all, of his customers. He functioned in rooms above a pool hall on Maryland Avenue.

Kennelly had seen many bookies. This one was not unique. It took different kinds of bets: on horses, on ball games, and on numbers. A teletype chattered away under a bell glass, bringing baseball information. On one wall, a huge blackboard displayed the scores. The bookie's son watched the tape and entered the results on the blackboard, not with chalk but with letters neatly numbered with a brush dipped in whitewash.

"Yankees been out a long time," a bettor observed. He meant that the score for the Yankee fifth inning had not been posted for half an hour, which suggested the Yankees were scoring. He would have liked to put a bet down on the Yankees, but it was too late now.

Race results came in by phone. A man wrote those on slips and posted them on a corkboard, where the bettors examined them.

The book was air cooled. A new invention dripped water over an absorbent filter in a machine that hung half outside the window. Air blowing across the wet filter evaporated the water and was cooled.

"Oh, man," the bookie complained. "What I done?"

"Nothing, 'Brose," said Kennelly. 'Brose meant Ambrose. "Not a thing at all. I just want you to look at a picture and tell me if you recognize the man."

'Brose shook his head mournfully. "Oh. Oh," he said when he looked at the picture. "That party *dead*, I hear! I got nothin' to do with that party gettin' dead!"

"I know you don't 'Brose. Where he got dead, you couldn't have been, and nobody you know could have been there either. You know what this guy did for a living?"

"He work in the White House. I hear he work in the White . . . *House*."

"He place his bets here?"

"Oh, man! I'm ethical. I don't—"

"So'm I," said Kennelly gruffly. "And Lieutenant Edward Kennelly, D.C. Homicide, can make it awful rough for a guy in your business."

'Brose nodded. "Reckon so," he said. "What is it you want to know, Ed?"

"Was this guy into you for more than he could pay?"

"Not into me. He bets with me, on the horses. But you know how this here business works. I lay them bets off to the layoff book. Man gets himself dead, he owes me somethin' like a hundred. But he owed the layoff book more like a thousand. There was *no way* that guy was gonna pay that off!"

"Would they kill him for it?"

"Sure. The business goes bust if we let guys get away with not payin'. *But in the White House!* You gotta be kiddin'!"

"The big guys must be against you, for letting it go that far."

"You don't understand the bookie business," said 'Brose. "Everything entirely depends on suckers bettin' more an' more an' more. More than they can afford, more than they can ever pay. We lose some. I mean, some never pay. But it works out on average. You don't make a profit by turnin' away suckers, tellin' them they credit's no good. Banks haven't figured it out yet, but we have. Lend, lend, lend! Money layin' around in you vault ain't makin' any money. We make our money work, and we win in the end."

"On the other hand, sometimes you lay a hit on a guy that doesn't pay."

"Not me, Sir! You know me better'n that, Ed."

6

"I WANT AN ANSWER," said Szczygiel. "I don't want any crappin' around. I want an answer."

He faced two uniformed officers of the White House police.

"Mr. Szczygiel—"

"I want a straightforward honest answer. How many you guys been foolin' around with Angie Patchen?"

"*Stan . . . !* For God's sake!"

"You?"

"No, Sir. As God is my witness."

"You?"

"No way. I got a wife and kids."

"Okay. How 'bout Doug?"

"Oh, well—"

"He had a wife and kids, too. But the answer is yes," Szczygiel concluded. "Right?"

"I don't like to—"

"The man was murdered," said Szczygiel sternly. "Now you guys tell me what you know about Angie and Doug."

"Okay. Doug had a case on her. I don't know if it ever came to . . . you know what. But he had a case on her."

"He talked about it?"

"He talked about it."

7

WHEN THE PRESIDENT CALLED out, "Who's home?" Missy came to the West Sitting Hall, as did Harry Hopkins and Joseph Kennedy. They sat down, a convivial group, and the president went through the ritual he so much enjoyed: mixing martinis as though he were a pharmacist preparing a prescription.

Kennedy did not mention the fact that he had met with the First Lady earlier. Is she had told the president, he knew it. If she had not, it wasn't Kennedy's place to advise him.

"I understand you've been yachting," said the president. "Did you meet a boat at sea and pick up some goodies?"

"Mr. President!"

"Well . . . did you? And did you bring something for me?"

"I'm afraid, Sir, that all we did was stock the bar of the yacht."

"With champagne for a wedding," said Missy sarcastically.

"As a matter of fact . . . yes, a lot of champagne."

"When is this wedding to take place?" asked the president.

"Soon, I gathered," said Kennedy.

"And who is marrying whom?" Missy asked.

"No one said."

"Are you invited?" the president asked.

"Not specifically. I gathered that I would be. But the date seems not to have been fixed."

"It may be on a cold day in hell," said Missy acerbically.

8

MRS. ROOSEVELT HAD A dinner engagement. The wives of the Democratic senators were meeting at the Madison Hotel, for a reception and dinner. She left the White House about seven and was driven to the hotel.

Prohibition remained the law, but almost no one paid it any attention. The reception was a cocktail party. The host was Vice President John Nance Garner, who somehow managed to smoke a big cigar and sip from a glass of bourbon with his left hand, leaving his right free to shake hands.

"Eleanor," he said as he pumped her arm, "by God, it is good to see you!"

He said the same to everyone—"good to *see* you." It was noncommital. He didn't say it was good to *meet* the person, since he might have met him or her before and the person might take offense that he did not remember. And, of course, saying it to someone he had already met was entirely appropriate. It was such a habit with him that he said it to the First Lady just as he did to everyone else.

Sam Rayburn was more subtle. He mumbled something that could be interpreted one way or another and won the person by his enthusiastic cordiality.

A woman shoved a glass of dry sherry toward Mrs. Roosevelt, and she accepted it and hoped no one would take notice that she was violating the Volstead Act just as Angela Patchen had done.

"I want you to meet someone," said the vice president. He beckoned to a small, shy man standing apart and looking lost. "Harry, come here and meet Mrs. Roosevelt."

The man came over and extended his right hand. He, too, was drinking bourbon, but he was not smoking a cigar.

"Eleanor, meet Harry Truman. He's a county judge in Jackson County, Missouri, and next year he's going to run for the Senate, and he's going to win. He'll be a big asset to the president."

"I am pleased to meet you, Mr. Truman. A judge—"

"Actually, Ma'am, I'm not a judge in the usual sense. County judge is what we in Missouri call the man who sees that roads are built and maintained and all like that—what you'd call a county commissioner in most states."

She studied this diffident country sort of man and wondered if he did not spend most of his days wearing bib overalls. His suit and his haircut suggested he did.

"Well, I shall be pleased to see you in the Senate," she said.

XIV

1

MRS. ROOSEVELT RETURNED TO the White House a little after nine-thirty. She went to the second floor on the West Elevator this time. As the elevator reached the second floor and before she could open the door, she heard the sickening, frightening sound of a shot. It was close by and had to be near the door to the president's bedroom. Heedless that it might be dangerous, she forced open the elevator door as soon as she could and ran into the Center Hall.

There, as she had feared, just outside the door to the president's bedroom, a man lay sprawled facedown on the floor. Another man stood a few feet from him, an automatic pistol in his right hand.

"My God! Mr. Szczygiel!"

Stanislaw Szczygiel turned calmly toward her, shoved the pistol into his shoulder holster, and said—"Our would-be assassin."

He pointed at the right hand of the sprawled man. It gripped a revolver.

The door to the president's bedroom opened, and Missy stood there in white peignoir and blue nightgown. She shrieked and retreated.

Mrs. Roosevelt approached the prone man. "He is . . . ?"

"I don't know," said Szczygiel.

"How did you . . . how did you happen to be here when—?"

"I've been here every night since the first attempt. I am relieved at midnight by a man I trust."

"Where is the uniformed officer who is supposed to be on duty here? Has he been—?"

"No. He's not here. And . . . and that would be Officer Hogan. He is not where he is supposed to be. I let him take his regular turn at this duty, even though I suspected him—knowing I would be here in case anything happened."

"I wasn't aware that you carry a gun. It is most fortunate that you do."

"I don't, ordinarily. I have been, these nights."

"And you were hidden . . . ?"

"In the guest room there," he said, nodding toward the door to a guest suite on the north side of the hall. "I carried a chair into the foyer and left the door ajar. Two of the officers on duty here have been thorough enough to discover me. Hogan was not."

"Are we to suppose that he stepped away from his

post to let this man approach the door to the president's bedroom?" she asked.

"I would like to hear what other explanation he has to offer."

Mrs. Roosevelt sighed heavily. "We . . . must call for a physician and—"

Szczygiel nodded, but he said, "The man is dead. I can promise you that."

The sound of the shot brought two uniformed officers to the Center Hall. Szczygiel ordered one of them to fetch the White House physician. He went to a telephone in the guest room and called Kennelly.

Missy opened the door to the president's bedroom, again, and stared at the man lying on the floor.

"Oh, my God! It's Nathan Clarke!"

2

MISSY RETURNED TO THE president, to help him into his wheelchair; and in a minute or so he rolled himself out. "So," he said. "It was not a mistake to take a look at this fellow."

"No," said Mrs. Roosevelt. "He came here to kill you, Franklin. And I think there is no doubt he is the one who did it last week."

"With help," said Szczygiel. Another Secret Service man had arrived, and Szczygiel gave him an order—"See to it that Officer Bob Hogan does not get out of the house and grounds."

"How did he get in?" the president asked.

"I'm afraid I know," said the First Lady. She shook her head sadly. "And I wish I didn't."

Missy had sunk to the floor and sat there crying. Mrs. Roosevelt stepped over to her and patted her head. The president wheeled himself to her and caressed her cheeks.

"He wanted to kill you, Effdee," Missy sobbed. "How could I have got rid of him? What could I have done?"

"It's not your fault," said the president gently.

"No, it wasn't," said Mrs. Roosevelt. "The man was mentally unbalanced."

Szczygiel knelt beside the body. "I don't care if the medical examiner hasn't seen him," he said. "I'm turning him over and going through his pockets."

The cause of Clarke's death was apparent. Szczygiel had shot him through the chest. His shirt and suit glistened with blood. It had soaked the carpet as well.

His mouth was wide open, as were his eyes. Szczygiel covered his face with a handkerchief. Mrs. Roosevelt and Missy didn't need to stare at that. The sight of the blood was bad enough.

Clarke's suit was cream-white and double-breasted. A dotted blue handkerchief stood in his breast pocket, nattily folded into three points. His shirt was light-blue silk. He wore two-tone shoes, tan and white.

Szczygiel pried the revolver from his hand. "Smith and Wesson," he said. "Thirty-eight. Deadly."

"What did you shoot him with, Brother Szczygiel?" the president asked.

"A nine-millimeter Luger," said Szczygiel. "A friend of mine brought it back from France in nineteen-nineteen and gave it to me. I don't know of a more accurate pistol."

He began to go through Clarke's pockets, tossing a billfold out on the floor, then a gold watch, then bills and change—finally a large key.

"Aha!" He turned to Mrs. Roosevelt. "I guess we expected that. Hmm?"

"I'm afraid we did."

"It's stamped with a number. We can easily find out who it was issued to."

"I think," said the First Lady, "it would be advisable if we assembled some people and held a conference."

"May I hope that Missy and I need not attend?" said the president.

"You need not," said Mrs. Roosevelt. "But after we check the number on that key, I will ask you to make a telephone call."

"Doug," said the president a few minutes later. "Don't ask how I knew where to call. I should be most grateful if you would make yourself available at the White House within the hour. A problem has arisen." *** "No, we're not being attacked." *** "I can't explain further now. You will be expected at the northwest gate, then at the security desk for the Executive Wing. There will be a meeting in the Cabinet Room."

3

ED KENNELLY AND D.C. officers had rounded up some people who had not expected to be summoned to the White House late on Friday night. Uniformed officers had detained Bob Hogan.

In the cabinet room, the people summoned assembled around the cabinet table. Mrs. Roosevelt presided at the head. The others sat around the table—

<table>
<tr><td colspan="2" align="center">Mrs. Roosevelt</td></tr>
<tr><td align="center">Stan Szczygiel</td><td align="center">Ed Kennelly</td></tr>
<tr><td align="center">General MacArthur</td><td align="center">Ben Hay</td></tr>
<tr><td align="center">Bob Hogan</td><td align="center">Angela Patchen</td></tr>
<tr><td align="center">Jo Pointer</td><td></td></tr>
<tr><td colspan="2" align="center">Stenographer</td></tr>
</table>

Hogan was in handcuffs, and an officer stood behind him. Other officers and Secret Service agents guarded the meeting.

"Ladies and gentlemen," said the First Lady, "tonight an attempt was made on the life of the president. It is the second such attempt within a week. Fortunately, neither attempt succeeded. Tonight the would-be assassin was killed just outside the door to the president's bedroom."

Angela had begun to cry. General MacArthur sat rigidly erect, the corners of his mouth turned down. He was wearing civilian dress: a dark-brown suit, and his boater straw hat lay on the table before him. Ben Hay and Jo Pointer were conspicuously nervous.

"The would-be assassin is dead. Some of you will know his name. He was Mr. Nathan Clarke."

Hay gasped. The general's face turned red.

The young woman at the stenotype pecked away, recording every word that was said, though not of course the reactions of the assembled people.

"Mr. Hay," said Mrs. Roosevelt, "you were our first suspect, indeed for several days our only suspect. I may tell you that your association with New York mobsters was of no help to you. You can now, if you wish, clear yourself finally of all suspicion, if you answer truthfully the questions we have to ask you."

"I have nothing to do with what happened here. I have nothing to hide."

"Then maybe you won't mind clearing up a few points," said the First Lady. "To begin with, would you mind telling us just what is the relationship between you and Mr. Arthur Flegenheimer?"

"Dutch Schultz," said Hay. "I met him through Dixie Davis, his lawyer. Dutch is a good-hearted guy who likes to make a variety of friends."

"I believe you were at a party at the establishment of Miss Polly Adler."

"Dutch's party," said Hay. "But he never showed up."

"Did Dutch ever lend you money?" asked Kennelly.

Hay nodded. "Several times."

"I guess you know some other people in the rackets," said Kennelly. "Luciano, Costello, Lansky, Buchalter, Anastasia . . . Right?"

"I'm acquainted with those fellows," said Hay.

"What is your salary as a government attorney?" asked Mrs. Roosevelt.

"Well . . . I suppose since it's a matter of record, I shouldn't take offense at the question. I make three thousand a year."

"But you live much more affluently than that figure would allow."

"I have other sources of income. My family—"

"Your family is only moderately prosperous," said Kennelly.

"A government lawyer is allowed to advise other clients, so long as it does not interfere with his work."

"So long as he doesn't disclose things he is not supposed to disclose," said the First Lady.

"There is another possibility," said Stan Szczygiel. "It has come up a number of times. During several administrations, employees have been caught using information they gained through their employment to suggest investments in the stock market. For example, in nineteen-thirty a man who was privy to the discussions about the Hawley-Smoot Tariff Bill used what he learned to invest in three companies that were going to benefit from tariff increases. He invested a thousand dollars and made four thousand within a few months. He didn't tell anybody else; he just used the information for himself."

"I was here. I remember," said Hay.

"Your brokerage account is in New York, I assume," said Szczygiel. "If we checked it, would we find that you invested ten thousand where the other man invested one?"

"It was not illegal," said Hay firmly. "I did not disclose anything. I just used the information for myself."

"It's called insider information," said Mrs. Roosevelt. "The new securities acts headed for Congress will make such trading illegal."

"Well, it's not now," said Hay defiantly.

"I am not so much interested in that question," said Szczygiel, "as I am interested in where you got the money to invest. Your three thousand a year didn't provide it."

"I have to wonder," said Mrs. Roosevelt, "if the money didn't come to you in the form of loans, or gifts, in return for which you *did* disclose to outsiders."

"Prove it," said Hay sullenly. "Anyway, I thought we were here to talk about why Nathan Clarke is dead."

"Did you know him?"

"I met him."

"One more question, then," said the First Lady. "Have you also met a young woman named Betty Nans?"

"Oh, no!" yelled Jo Pointer.

"Did you have to bring *that* up?" Hay demanded angrily. "There's no limit to you New Dealers, is there?"

"It has come to our attention, Miss Pointer, that you, too, are acquainted with some of the Mob figures in New York City."

Jo Pointer began to sob quietly. "Sure," she whispered. "I came to New York. I had money. I went places where people could get in with money and nothing else. So . . . I started hanging around at the Stork Club. I met all the big crooks. Billingsley. Winchell. Lansky. Siegel. I met them because the real celebrities didn't want to meet me. Ben Siegel asked me for a date, and I went out with him four times. Never call him Bugsy, incidentally. He'll break your nose."

"Your money came from Detroit," said Mrs. Roosevelt.

"From my father. He sends me an allowance, provided only that I stay away from him and the rest of the family. He also gave me a thousand shares of his company."

"Nans—"

"My mother's name was Nan. That made me Nans. It was like a blinking sign over my head, screaming, *Bastard, bastard, bastard!* I started calling myself Pointer. It refers to Grosse Pointe. If you think that tells you who I am, remember that lots of very wealthy people live in Grosse Pointe."

"Did Nathan Clarke give you presents?" Lieutenant Kennelly asked. He was thinking about the cigarette case engraved *JP from NC.*

"Nat gave everybody presents," she said. "He hoped to make people like him. Nobody was going to if he didn't."

"Well then, Hogan," said Kennelly. "Where were you when Clarke approached the door of the president's bedroom?"

"I had to go to the men's room," said Hogan.

"You are supposed to be sure your post is covered when you do that," said Szczygiel.

"I was only gonna be gone a minute."

"A significant minute," said Mrs. Roosevelt.

"It had got urgent," said Hogan. "I came close to having an accident."

"You paid Harrigan fifty dollars," said Szczygiel. "You were going to pay McKay another fifty. That's a lot of money for a night with Angie."

"The girl is worth it."

Angela had been crying softly all along. Now she sobbed deeply, and her eyes flooded with tears.

"Clarke entered the White House to assassinate the president," said Kennelly. "You didn't let him in. After midnight you could have opened the west gate with your key, but the gate was still guarded by Harrigan when Doug Douglas was killed. To open a gate and let a man in was too much for what you were paying Harrigan. He said it himself. There's a world of difference between fudging a log to help a fellow officer shack up with—"

"Excuse me, Mrs. Roosevelt."

"I should have used exactly the same words myself," she said.

Kennelly went on. "Between that and violating the integrity of White House security."

"He paid you that much money because someone was paying him," said Mrs. Roosevelt. "I believe we know that Mr. Clarke splashed money around recklessly."

"How'd you meet Clarke, Hogan?" Kennelly asked.

"I never did."

"Bob!" shrieked Angela. "They got us cold! They got us cold!"

"Shut up! Nobody's got anybody!"

The girl covered her face with her hands and dropped it to the table with a thud. She shook with sobs.

"Okay, Bob. Apparently you *did* know Clarke," said Ed Kennelly coldly. "How? Where'd you meet him?"

"Tell him about Doug," Angela muttered through her hands.

"Bitch," grunted Hogan.

"There was going to be big money," she murmured. "We were supposed to get real big money. See . . . Doug owed—"

"Okay," Hogan snapped. "The bitch would never get it straight. So, okay, Doug Douglas was into this bookie for more than he could ever hope to pay. And he was gettin' pressed. Not by the nigger in the bookie. By the layoff guys. They're tough. Doug was scared to death. So this guy comes to him and says he'll cover Doug's bets if Doug'll do somethin' for him. This was Nat, Nat Clarke."

"In Washington?" asked the First Lady.

"Nat got around. He was from New York, but he had some reason to be in Washington. Where he went, he always met with the big guys. Like Meyer Lansky, who's got a carpet joint over in Virginia. They were buddies in New York, buddies here. I guess he got it from Lansky that a White House cop was on the arm for big money."

"Go on."

"So Nat sees Doug and tells him he'll bail him out if Doug will do somethin' for him. But Doug—" Hogan paused and shook his head. "Doug said he'd do anything he could, so long as it didn't involve his duties in the White House." Hogan sneered. "Why did he think Nat would bail him out?"

"Only if he facilitated an attempt to assassinate the president," said Mrs. Roosevelt.

Hogan nodded. "Okay. Doug tells me this story. I figure he's throwin' away the opportunity of a lifetime. So I went to see Bobby Asman, and she told me how to get in touch with Lansky. I did, and Lansky put me in touch with Nat."

"Then they got *me* involved," wept Angela.

"Okay," Hogan went on. "I guess I might as well tell you this. You got it all figured out anyway. Doug had hots for Angie. We put her in a guest room across the Center Hall—stark naked. I was watching from the Stair Hall. When I saw Nat come up the stairs, I ran down to the

East Room and used the phone there to ring the phone in the room where Angie was waiting. I let it ring just once. That was her signal. She stepped out into the Center Hall, all naked, and while Doug stared at her, Nat ran up to him and stabbed him."

"Then he was to break into the president's bedroom and stab the president," said Mrs. Roosevelt somberly.

"Right. Only the president had guests. Nat could hear their voices: two or three men. He turned around and scrammed."

"And that's all I had to do with it," sobbed Angela.

"And tonight?" asked Szczygiel.

Hogan shrugged. "This time he came with a gun. Nobody figured that Mr. Szczygiel would be waiting with his own gun."

Mrs. Roosevelt sighed. "Which leaves us with a few questions. How did Mr. Clarke get into the White House—and out again after he killed Officer Douglas? How did he expect to get out tonight?" She turned and faced General MacArthur.

"I suppose I am the one in trouble now," said General MacArthur in a deep, calm voice. "I guessed I was when the president called me at the Hotel Chastleton. He was not supposed to know about that."

"No one is supposed to know about it, General," said the First Lady.

"Very well," said General MacArthur. "He let himself in and out of the White House through the Treasury Tunnel, using my key. I was issued a key to that gate. Chiefs of staff always are. Sometimes it is important for us to come and go without being seen. I allowed Nathan Clarke to use my key. What can I say? I swear before God Almighty that I had no notion whatever that he was coming here to attempt to assassinate the president. He cited a very different reason."

"Which was?"

"He was deeply in love with Marguerite LeHand, Missy. He thought if he could visit her, in her bedroom, he could persuade her to accept his proposal of marriage. He knew she spent her evenings with the president. He meant to be waiting for her when she came up to her suite."

"The man was a nut," Jo Pointer muttered.

"You were—are—deeply in debt to Nathan Clarke," said Mrs. Roosevelt.

"Now that he is dead I am not," the general said coldly. "I signed no notes. He never asked me to."

"He imagined he would get what he wanted," said the First Lady.

"He used his money extravagantly," said General MacArthur.

"And not always wisely," said Mrs. Roosevelt. "The man was *stupid!* If he had shot the president this evening, he would have had to shoot Missy. She was there. If he had broken in with his bayonet, he would have had to kill her, too."

"Knowing him as I did," said the general, "I have to suspect he imagined she would *admire* him—a man who would kill for her love. I suppose he thought he would take her out through the tunnel and rush her to his yacht. He probably thought he would be anchored in the lagoon in Venice before anyone got it all figured out."

"He was a *nut*," said Jo Pointer.

"Presidential assassins and would-be assassins generally have been," said Mrs. Roosevelt.

EPILOGUE

IT WAS IMPERATIVE THAT the events just outside the president's bedroom be kept secret. The participants benefited from that necessity.

The president did not dismiss General Douglas MacArthur from his job as chief of staff, U.S. Army. He took note that the general had been guilty of lapses of judgment, and he would always remember that fact and keep a tight reign over the man who came to be called the American Caesar.

Isabel Rosario Cooper remained General MacArthur's mistress only a short time longer. The scandal journalist Drew Pearson wrote a column about the relationship, General MacArthur sued for libel, and the case was settled without further scandal. Isabel moved away from Washington, living for a while on proceeds from the settlement. She died in California in 1946.

Ben Hay resigned as a government attorney and returned to New York, where he married Betty Nans: Jo

Pointer. They lived handsomely on her allowance. When her father died and her allowance ceased, she sold her thousand shares in his corporation for more than three million dollars and invested the proceeds carefully. Hay became a lawyer for various members of the New York Five Families. He was disbarred in 1947, and the couple moved to St. Tropez, on the French Riviera, where they lived in a villa until their deaths in the 1970s

In 1934 Dutch Schultz was shot to death in a New Jersey café by gunmen from Murder Incorporated. He had ordered the death of District Attorney Thomas Dewey, and the Families would not tolerate things like that.

Lucky Luciano served time in a New York prison on prostitution charges. He cooperated with the government in securing waterfront peace during World War II and was released and deported to Italy, where he struggled for years to be readmitted to the United States. Lepke Buchalter died in the electric chair at Sing Sing. Bugsy Siegel was largely instrumental in establishing Mob investment in Las Vegas. He was shot to death in his girlfriend's apartment in the late 1940s: a Mob hit because he had become too notorious. Albert Anastasia was shot and killed in a barber chair in a New York hotel in the 1960s: Mob war. Meyer Lansky died in bed in the 1970s.

Lieutenant Ed Kennelly was in time promoted to captain and would assist the First Lady in several other criminal investigations.

Stan Szczygiel kept trying to retire but was prevented

by various exigencies and remained a senior agent of the Secret Service until his late seventies.

Office Robert Hogan was sentenced to twenty-five years in prison. He served six years in Leavenworth, where he proved so troublesome that he was transferred to Alcatraz in 1940. He was released in 1958, aged fifty-nine. In 1960 he was arrested for auto theft, and sentenced to ten years in Illinois. He died in prison in 1968.

Angela Patchen was sentenced to ten years. She was released from the federal reformatory for women in 1943, aged forty. She became a prostitute and died of venereal disease in 1955.

By then, Mrs. Roosevelt no longer lived in the White House.

Murder at the President's Door
AFicRo
30459000196611
Roosevelt, Elliot